Fire and Honor
The Lightwood Affair Book 1

By M. S. Parker

This book is a work of fiction. The names, characters, places and incidents are products of the writer's imagination or have been used fictitiously and are not to be construed as real. Any resemblance to persons, living or dead, actual events, locales or organizations is entirely coincidental.
Copyright © 2016 Belmonte Publishing
Published by Belmonte Publishing.

ISBN-13: 978-1541361201
ISBN-10: 1541361202

Table of Contents

Table of Contents 3
Chapter 1 1
Chapter 2 12
Chapter 3 23
Chapter 4 30
Chapter 5 41
Chapter 6 47
Chapter 7 56
Chapter 8 65
Chapter 9 73
Chapter 10 81
Chapter 11 89
Chapter 12 98
Chapter 13 107
Chapter 14 115
Chapter 15 126
Chapter 16 135
Chapter 17 144
Chapter 18 155
Chapter 19 166
Chapter 20 177
Chapter 21 185
Chapter 22 191
Chapter 23 197

Chapter 24	205
Chapter 25	215
Chapter 26	223
Chapter 27	231
Chapter 28	237
Chapter 29	246
More from M.S. Parker	251
Acknowledgement	252
About the Author	253

Chapter 1

The bullet grazed my shoulder seconds before I realized what was happening, burning a path across my skin.

The noise around me was deafening. Automatic gunfire mixing with shouts in English and whatever dialect of Arabic our assailants were using. A hand pushed my head down, and my entire body slipped into the front floorboard as bullets slammed against the SUV's shell.

Shit!

"Get us out of here!" I snapped the order even as my brain was still registering the fact that what should've been a simple mission had turned into a shit-storm.

I looked up at Wilkins as he slammed on the gas, throwing all of us backwards. I tried to push myself up, already reaching for my weapon, but he shoved me down again. I glared at him but didn't try to move. He needed both his hands to drive, and I'd only be a distraction.

"Chew my ass out all you want when we get back to base, but for now, stay the hell down," he yelled, maneuvering the vehicle expertly as shots ricocheted off the SUV.

I didn't get up, but I did turn so I could see the rest

of my team. Rogers was in the backseat, his hand on his side as I watched the blood stain his shirt. Instincts to serve and protect over-rode natural self-preservation, and I started to push myself up.

"Dammit, Honor, get your sexy ass down!" Wilkins shouted. "You can't help him if you're dead. I need ten minutes."

"He doesn't have ten minutes!" I shot back, shoving gauze against my own flesh wound. It wasn't the first time Wilkins felt the need to protect me just because I was a woman. I can take on this war just as good as any man.

Wilkins quickly glanced behind him, cursed under his breath, and pushed down harder on the gas. Rogers groaned in pain as we hit a speed bump, but he shook his head at me when I leaned forward. Damn him and his ability to read what I was thinking. I gritted my teeth, my impatience making my fear secondary even though gunshots were still ringing around us.

As we moved out of range, Wilkins didn't slow, but he did gesture for me to move. I quickly jumped into the back seat, grabbing for my medic kit as I went. I picked up a pair of scissors and cut the hole in Rogers' shirt so I could get a better look at his wound. Working quickly, I caught Wilkins' eyes in the rearview mirror and glared at him before turning back to Rogers.

"Will he be okay?" Wilkins asked as he took another hairpin turn.

I ignored the question, keeping my mind on the task at hand as the SUV bumped from side to side on what passed for a road here.

"That was a little unexpected," Wilkins ventured.

I shot him another look, and this time, I couldn't keep my mouth shut. "This was the stupidest thing I've ever seen you do, Wilkins!"

"That's saying something," Rogers gasped out. His

face was pale, and I had a feeling he was distracting himself.

"It was recon," Wilkins argued.

"It was miles away from where we should have been," I shot back. "I'm okay with dying for my country, but I don't want it to be because my driver was off doing his own thing."

Rogers put a hand on mine and managed a grin. "No one's dying here, corporal."

I could see how much pain he was in, but the fact that he could smile and was taking the time to reassure me helped me relax. Or, at least as much as I could relax over here.

I hardly ever slept.

It wasn't insomnia, per say, just the combination of adrenaline and my thoughts, which I had come to learn was never a good thing. Still, there was some consolation in being the only one up at an hour when everyone around was fast asleep. Things usually seemed clearer then, thoughts more discernible, and sometimes, I eventually got a couple hours of sleep.

Iraq was taking its toll on me. Hell, it took its toll on everyone, but I thought being a military brat had helped me be prepared. It hadn't. But I'd done my duty. Six years in the army, having enlisted right out of high school, and I started to think I was ready to go home. Ready to be a civilian. The thought of opening my own pediatric practice was the only thing that seemed to make me smile these days. Still, I knew that I'd done the right thing by enlisting.

I kept pressure on Rogers' side until we pulled into the base camp, then yelled for some help. I was tall and strong enough to pass the physical part of being an army medic with flying colors. Rogers, however, was a giant and I doubted most men would be able to carry him without assistance. Less than two minutes later, we were in the infirmary and Rogers was getting the attention he needed.

I made my way down the dim hall, automatically blocking out the chaotic noise coming at me from all sides. I'd gotten used to the military atmosphere early on, my dad bringing home a small part of the army with him even after he retired. He ran the house like his own little unit, and to me, it had always been like I was part of something bigger than just my immediate family.

I recalled late nights on the couch with my brother while our father sat in his favorite chair, telling us stories about the army, our eyes wide with awe. Ennis had enlisted too, of course. It was how our family had put themselves through college for years. I'd never doubted that I'd do the same.

I stopped at Captain Riley Nolan's office, knocking lightly, and walking in when the call came for me to enter. I saluted and stood at attention.

"At ease, corporal," Nolan said, his pen dancing across the sheet of paper in front of him as he worked.

I watched the man work for another few minutes, admiring how easy it was for him to simply forget everyone around him and focus on one task after the other. I'd never come across Nolan and found him sitting around gazing at the sky, lost in his thoughts, pondering the meaning of the universe. If there was one man on earth who could pound a soldier into the ground with assignments, it was Nolan, and his ruthlessness matched his work ethics.

He reminded me of my dad.

"I hear you had a small run-in this afternoon," Nolan said as he sat back in his seat, his blue eyes boring into mine.

"We ran across some militia," I explained. "Nothing serious."

"I heard Rogers got shot," Nolan said. "You too. That seems pretty serious to me."

I hesitated, wondering just how much the captain had already heard, and how much he expected me to tell him. Wilkins had gone off route, and that wouldn't be easy to explain. I was stuck between not wanting to sell out Wilkins, and needing to tell my captain the truth.

Loyalty seemed like a simple enough concept until things went sideways.

"Mine was only a graze, and Rogers is patched up, ready to go, sir," I said, choosing to go with Nolan's most recent comment rather than what I knew he wanted to hear.

I let out a slow breath and eased when the captain nodded and sat up straight in his chair, his hands fluttering through pages on his desk as he looked for something. I waited, wondering if that would be all when he held up a paper and handed it to me.

"You're going home, corporal," he said as I reached out and took the order. "The entire unit, two weeks. Let them know."

I nodded, trying my best to hide my smile and saluted again. I turned to leave when he spoke. "Tell Wilkins to get some good rest on leave, Daviot. We don't want him stressed and incapable of following orders."

"Will do, sir," I answered before walking out.

"So, will Bruce be waiting at the airport for you?" Rogers asked. He wagged his eyebrows. "Gonna get him some lovin'..."

I smacked him, then immediately regretted it when he groaned in pain.

"Sorry," I chuckled. "Are you alright?"

"You're not sorry," Rogers said, laughing as he pushed me away. He got up and stretched, feeling at his stitches as I went back to packing my bags.

Wilkins threw me a look. "You didn't answer his question."

"I left Bruce a message," I said, trying to hide the fact that my fiancé's inability to answer his cell phone was starting to get on my nerves. It wasn't like we had that much free time out here that we could pick and choose when we wanted to chat.

"A message," Wilkins repeated, glancing at Rogers. "Do you hear that, Rogers? She left lover boy a message."

I shot Wilkins a dangerous look. He laughed and raised his hands in surrender.

"Hey, don't get me wrong, but if it was my fiancée calling after months apart, I'd as sure as hell answer that call on the first ring," he said, laughing.

"Mind your own business," I shot back, a half-smile creeping onto my face. "At least he's not trying to get me killed."

Wilkins had the decency to look embarrassed.

Rogers sat down on my bed and stretched his legs in front of him. He seemed quite spry, despite the fact that he had just been shot and had a big ass bullet yanked out. It always impressed me how much of a beating he could take and still keep going.

"I'm looking forward to steak dinners," he said, changing the subject as he looked up at the ceiling with a smile.

"A good old Mickey D's burger, that's what I want," Wilkins chimed in. "I don't care what poison they've got in that thing, I'm going to eat enough of them to last through my next deployment."

I thought back to my mom's roast, the dinner table set up so the entire family could enjoy the meal. Being away made the little things more precious, made me realize how much I'd taken for granted growing up.

"How about you, Daviot? What's the first thing you want to eat when you get home?"

I thought about it for a minute and couldn't really narrow things down to one preference. I just wanted to get home. I had two months left before I had to decide whether or not I planned to re-enlist, and I'd been debating about it for the past couple weeks. I wanted to get married, finish my degree, open my own pediatric practice and leave the war behind me. I was done fighting, or at least I thought I was, the uncertainty in my mind like a dark cloud of what-ifs and maybes. No matter how many times I tried to make a decision, I was always overwhelmed with the responsibility of making the *right* choice.

My mother had started a tradition when I was in the seventh grade. After dinner, we'd all share our problems, dilemmas, basically anything that bothered us. We talked things over, weighed pros and cons, asked for advice. Granted, we didn't always share things we considered embarrassing, but we'd always done our best to try to help with whatever issue was presented.

Going home might actually make things easier, even if I had a feeling my father would want me to stay in the army.

"Not sure," I finally said. "A good drink, maybe?"

Wilkins smiled. "Ah, girls' night out. Maybe I should come to Boston with you."

"Well, it wouldn't be a girls' night without you, would it?" I shot at him.

"There will come a day, Daviot, when you'll realize that I'm the only man in the world for you," Wilkins teased.

I gave him the finger and then smiled as Rogers fell back and laughed, each one punctuated with winces of pain.

"I never really understood long distance relationships," Wilkins went on. "Why not just have an open thing so you could hook up with whoever you wanted. Come to think of it, I should get one of those. Maybe even two or three."

"You're disgusting, you know that?" I shot at him, smiling despite myself.

"Come on, Daviot, you know I'm right." Wilkins shrugged. "Long distance relationships never work out."

I glared at him as I zipped my carry-on shut. We had an early flight out, so I wanted to get some shut eye. If I could.

Turns out, I could. I slept that night, and I dreamed.

I hadn't dreamed in years, or at least none that I could remember. I was usually too tired that when I finally did sleep, my body shut completely down when it couldn't take being awake any longer. Insomnia trumped all. There was rarely time for dreams.

Tonight was different though. I was in a field, a large one, somewhere I didn't recognize, dressed in clothes I'd never worn, running between men with muskets as mounds of earth blew up into the air. I could feel the adrenaline coursing through me, the urgency in my step.

I glanced back at the men running behind me, each muddy and clearly tired, though pushing on with dogged ferocity. My entire body shivered with excitement, and I pressed on with them.

In my dream, something exploded beside me, throwing me to the ground even as it woke me.

I looked around, sweating, shivering, and squinting as I tried to calm the pounding in my chest, the breaths that were coming in gasps. I barely registered the sleeping bodies of my unit, squinting in the darkness as I tried to wrap my head around what I'd just experienced. It had been so vivid, so real.

I laid back down and covered my eyes with my arm. I needed sleep, but I wasn't sure if I'd get anymore tonight.

Chapter 2

I touched down at Logan Airport with a genuine smile on my face. The idea of finally being home had truly hit me when we'd crossed into Massachusetts. I was home. As the captain announced our descent, he added that it was a beautiful June afternoon, and then thanked the service men and women who were on board. The heat was still in my cheeks as I exited the plane. I liked knowing that my service was appreciated, but I'd never really liked being put on the spot.

I was looking forward to seeing my parents and brother, but at the moment, just being on home soil was enough. It'd been almost a year since the last time I was stateside, and if I decided not to re-enlist, I'd most likely never experience this again.

One of the best things about being part of a military family was that I knew they understood how I felt. I called my brother to tell him the good news, and it was nice not to have to try to explain things like I would have if Bruce had picked up his phone.

Ennis also never edged around the tough questions, but rather asked flat-out if I'd made a decision about joining civilian life. He also understood how difficult the decision was. Two years older than me, he'd taken the plunge first, deciding to pursue his doctorate in education with a focus in American history. Our dad had taken it better than Ennis and I thought he would. Now, it was my turn, and I was glad to know that my brother had my back.

I just wished my fiancé was as understanding.

I called Bruce two more times, both times leaving a voice message about my leave because he hadn't picked up. It was hurtful, I had to admit, that he didn't go out of his way to answer my calls. We'd known each other for so long, had dated on and off since junior high. We'd been friends even before that. It was hard enough that he never supported my tours without him completely ignoring my calls.

Wilkins had told me more than once that Bruce was a lost cause, and lately, I'd begun to believe it. We'd been exclusive to each other since we were sixteen, engaged by nineteen. He'd been the only one for me, but since I'd enlisted, I had a feeling that things were one-sided on that account. I'd never confronted him about it, but recently, I had to admit that part of the reason I'd stayed quiet was because I didn't want to hear the answer. I just couldn't deal with that kind of a discussion and still function optimally in battle.

I could almost hear the excuses he'd make if I did ask. He made them about other things often enough.

You're never around. You're off playing hero. I have my needs.

It always made my blood boil to hear him talk like that, but I couldn't deny that strengthening my relationship with Bruce was one of the reasons I was thinking of not re-enlisting. I kept telling myself that things would be better when I was home full time.

My seatmate kept up a steady stream of chatter as we stepped out into the main concourse where she was smothered by a man double my size. I smiled at them, watching various other passengers share welcomes with those waiting for them. I looked around for Bruce but couldn't find him in the crowd.

I frowned as I looked at my phone again, wondering if I'd missed his call. Nope. Nothing there. I double-checked to make sure I'd turned off airplane mode, then scowled as I wondered if he'd forgotten about the flight, even though I'd sent him a text message to remind him of the time and gate number. What was the point of having a cell phone if he didn't answer?

When it came to being there for me, Bruce needed to step up his game. I didn't really feel like spending the rest of my life with someone who could so easily forget that I even existed. Not showing up at the airport was just one more time he'd let me down.

I decided to step back a bit, giving him the benefit of the doubt, already feeling the fatigue setting in. At some point, I'd have to trust that he would come through. I was just waiting for the day for that to actually happen.

By the time Bruce finally answered my call, I was sitting in the airport coffee shop with my bags and a hot cup of cappuccino in front of me, regretting not taking up my brother's offer to have him skip his classes and pick me up.

When I heard Bruce slur his greeting, as if he was just now waking up, I forced myself to swallow my anger.

"Hey, it's me."

"Honor?"

"Yeah," I said, taking a sip from my coffee, savoring the flavor. "Where are you?"

"I'm in bed," Bruce coughed. "Why?"

Annoyance flared. What the hell? It was the middle of the afternoon. "You didn't get my messages? Any of them?"

"What messages?"

I gritted my teeth. "I'm at the airport, Bruce, waiting for you to pick me up."

"You're what?" He suddenly seemed wide awake. "When did you get there?"

"*There*?" I asked, ignoring the question. "What do you mean by *there*? Where are you?"

He hesitated before answering, "I'm in Vegas, Honor. I took some vacation time and flew out yesterday. I'm sure I told you."

It took every ounce of energy and willpower to keep my voice level. "You can't be serious?! I have leave for two weeks, and you're in Vegas? I called you three times in the past two days. Why didn't you pick up?"

"Damn, take it easy, babe. I didn't see them." He sounded more annoyed than I thought he had the right to be. "But, hey, since you're still in the airport, just hop on a plane and come here. You'd love the room."

I sighed heavily, trying to calm myself down. "I just got in, Bruce. I'm not about to jump on another plane."

"Why not? You're already jet lagged. You could catch a few hours of sleep on the trip."

I closed my eyes. I shouldn't have to explain this to him. "I've already been in the air for more than twelve hours. I'm not getting on a six-hour flight to Vegas just because you forgot about me."

Hot tears pricked at my eyelids, and I took a shaking breath in an effort to keep them back. Fatigue and frustration were doing a number on my usual composure.

"Listen, I'm sorry, I really am," he said, his voice

turning sexy and low. "I had no idea. Please, just get on a plane and come here. Spend your leave with me. We can get married in Vegas, baby. Isn't that what you always wanted? An exotic wedding?"

"Having Elvis marry us isn't my idea of exotic, Bruce." My head was starting to pound.

There were times when arguing with Bruce was completely useless. I blamed it on the fact that, for the past seven years, we'd spent ninety percent of our time together in different states. Sometimes different continents.

I remember Rogers once telling me that he admired how well we were keeping a long distance relationship going. It was times like this that I wondered how functional that relationship even was.

"Okay, seriously, give me a break already." Bruce broke into my thoughts. "I thought you wanted to get married. Isn't that why we're engaged in the first place?"

I bristled. "We're getting married because we want to, not because you're trying to make it up to me."

"Make what up to you?" Bruce shot back. "I had no idea you were coming back today, Honor. Let it go."

"I called you three times!" My frayed temper boiled over, and I knew I was talking too loud. "Left three messages and half a dozen texts. You couldn't bother to check your phone?"

"I was busy," he argued, his voice full of anger.

"You're in Vegas! What the hell is keeping you busy?"

"Stop shouting," he snapped. "I don't need this right now."

He didn't need this?

"I just got back from Iraq, Bruce. Iraq. You're an investment banker in Boston who's on vacation in

Vegas. I'm the one who doesn't need this. All I wanted was to come home to my family and spend some quality time with my fiancé before I had to hop on a plane back to hell!"

"You're going back?"

I was suddenly glad that he wasn't here, because if he'd said that to my face, I probably would have hit him. I struggled to lower my voice. "Have you not listened to a single word I've said?"

There was an awkward silence that lasted forever as each one of us waited for the other to speak. When it was apparent that neither of us would break the silence, I hung up before I would say something I regretted.

For the first time since I'd known him, I hated Bruce.

My hands shook as I stared into my coffee and tried to get my temper under control. I had no idea how much more of this I was willing to take. Long distance relationships were hard enough, and I didn't need the extra stress of a fiancé who couldn't care enough to work at it.

The phone in my hand rang, and I didn't need to look at the caller ID to know it was Bruce. He'd probably come up with a dozen other ways of how this was my fault. Enlisting when he'd made it clear that wasn't what he wanted made everything since that moment my fault. I let it go to voicemail and tried my best to compose myself. I didn't want to break down completely. Not here. I needed to pull my shit together myself enough to decide if I wanted to wait for Ennis to be done with his classes, call my parents, or rent a car. Right now though, I couldn't think.

The third time he called, I answered just so he wouldn't keep calling.

"Come to Vegas," he said without any preamble.

"Come to Vegas and let's get married."

He really didn't get it. He thought asking me to fly out to see him and change our status from engaged to married would fix what was broken between us.

"I can't, Bruce." The fatigue I felt before settled even deeper into my bones. "I need to think about a lot of things. I need to rest. I need to go home and see my family. Talk to them about what I want to do."

I didn't mention talking to him about decisions influencing my future. *My* future. I sighed. I didn't even think of it as *our* future.

"Just get on a plane, babe," he said. "I'll pay for it."

"It's not the mon–" I started but realized that whatever I said right now, it would just go right over his head. I sighed. "I'll try and book a flight out on Saturday."

"Why wait until Saturday?" He sounded petulant, like a child rather than a twenty-five-year-old man. "You said it yourself. You could be here in six hours, not two days."

Ennis once said that Bruce was one of those people who thought the world revolved around them and didn't understand why anyone would want to do anything other than what he wanted. Over the past couple years, I'd seen that side of Bruce more than I cared to admit.

"I'll call you later tonight." I hung up before we started shouting at each other again.

It took me another hour to get up from my seat, mostly because it took that long for my brain to quiet down. I called my parents and let them know that I'd be renting a car and driving out. Neither of them seemed surprised that Bruce hadn't shown up. I didn't tell them about Vegas. They already weren't fond of my fiancé. I didn't need to add any additional fuel to that particular fire.

Now that I'd decided what to do about transportation, I quickly found the closest Budget Rental, filled out the paperwork and gave the man behind the counter my driver's license. He asked me about my trip, and when he found out I was stationed in Iraq, started bombarding me with questions. Apparently, his cousin was stationed there too. I didn't recognize the name but let him carry on a one-sided conversation while he entered my information into the computer.

I took the keys and made my way outside, led by the man as he started to talk about why he couldn't enlist, as if he owed me some kind of explanation. By the time I was behind the wheel and driving away, the throbbing in my temples had turned into a full-blown headache.

I needed real food and sleep. Like two days' worth of both.

My parents had a small house outside the city, a suburban haven where my father felt he was farthest away from the noise. After a childhood of moving from base to base, I'd been thrilled when we'd moved into a permanent residence.

I'd often talked to Bruce about buying our own place in the same neighborhood, but he'd always shot the idea down. He'd grown up three houses down the street, but he now said he needed the life of the city to thrive. It was funny that how, only now, I was starting to clearly see the things I'd ignored about him before.

It wasn't like me to keep my head in the sand, to refuse to address what was right in front of me. I pressed my fingers to my temple. Why now? Why him? Was I so desperate to achieve my happy ever after that I'd clung stubbornly to the one man I'd always thought would share it with me?

Every argument we ever had came rushing back. It was like my mind was re-playing everything for me, hinting at the fact that maybe, just maybe, it was about time to let this whole thing go. To let Bruce go. The thought of it made my stomach turn, but another part of me realized this was merely a prequel to the emotions I would feel if I actually went through with it.

Maybe him not being here was for the best. Besides, I needed to spend time with my parents.

It was only when I was on McClellan Highway that I finally rolled the window down and breathed in the Boston air. The Chelsea River whispered at me from my left, and I let out every ounce of negative energy inside me, finally allowing myself to smile. Bruce could wait, I thought to myself. For now, it was just good to be home.

The screeching to my right yanked me from my pleasant thoughts, and I turned my head to see a blue sedan spin out of control. I slammed on the brakes and swerved, hoping to avoid a collision as I cut across the highway. I waited for the impact, but it never came. My car's front bumper barely missed the other car as it skidded and flipped.

Before I could swerve back, the loud screams of a horn told me the danger wasn't over. My turn had me right in the middle of oncoming traffic and drivers who were going too fast to stop. In front of me, a truck was trying to brake hard, but I knew there wasn't enough room.

I braced myself as the truck slammed into my car, the force bending the driver's side inwards, the window and windshield showering me with safety glass. I closed my eyes to protect them, my hands holding tight onto the steering wheel as the entire car turned. Before I knew what was happening, I was upside down, the truck's tires screaming behind me, my rental flipping once, twice, three times, until it slammed down on its wheels.

I heard more screeching, and somewhere in the distance, a crash that told me things weren't over yet. It was going to be a pileup, and the only thing I could think of as I sat strapped into my seat, unable to move, was that these people would need a doctor and that I was the first on the scene.

The world went fuzzy then, and I heard someone shouting in the distance. My eyes opened and closed as I tried to stay conscious. I felt a hand grab my shoulder, barely registering the man shouting at me, asking if I was okay. I looked at him, frowning as his face seemed to flicker and change. He tried to unlock my seatbelt, and for a second I saw the whole world around me shift, saw my car and the road disappear, morph into an empty, open field. And then things went back to the real world. Cars and blood and noise.

"Can you move your legs?" the man asked me.

I mumbled something incoherent, trying to tell him that he was working the wrong seat belt, when the entire world around me darkened, blurred. The last thing I felt were his hands under my shoulders, trying to pull me out of the car, and then...

Nothing at all.

Chapter 3

I was never much of a believer in anything supernatural or paranormal.

It had nothing to do with upbringing since my parents were both Catholics. They'd raised Ennis and me in the church, but it had mostly consisted of baptisms and holidays. They hadn't been overly religious, but if asked, they'd both have said they believe in God.

I never had, not really. Maybe once I'd believed in the concept of a general higher power. Then I went to Iraq. The deaths I saw, the sheer incomprehensible darkness that man had towards one another, well, it made what belief I'd possessed falter.

Maybe that was why I couldn't understand what was happening.

At one point, I thought I saw a bright light, something along the lines of a tunnel, like the kind of images people talked about when they died. Then, in a flash, it was gone, replaced by only darkness and flashing lights, different colors, each blinking long enough to capture my attention, making me turn my head towards it before being captivated by another.

"Honor?"

I turned my head towards the voice, the image of

Bruce materializing out of the darkness. The smile he'd always used to win me over flashed across his face as he seemed to float towards me, hand outstretched, welcoming.

"Come to Vegas," Bruce said.

I frowned at him, and just like that, he disappeared. It was like his entire being broke apart into tiny particles that blew away as if he'd been made of pure dust that sparkled and shone as it flew around me in a whirlwind of tiny colors.

"Who are you?"

Another voice, one I couldn't make out. Far away, yet close at the same time. I felt a pressure on my shoulders, and then it was gone. I was floating in an ocean of nothingness, my legs kicking out slowly. I remembered videos of astronauts in space and how they floated about their space stations in zero gravity and wondered if this was how they felt.

Was this what death was like? Was I in space?

"Honor?"

I looked around, swimming to adjust the rest of my body toward where the sound was coming from. I saw Bruce again, but he was younger now, the boy I'd first met before sixth grade. He was barely eleven then, with his ruffled hair, Pacman t-shirt, and high-tops, sitting on his BMX as he looked at me.

I smiled at him, but he didn't smile back. He was looking past me at someone else, and before I could turn my head to see who, a little girl ran past me. Dressed in jeans, and a ridiculous green shirt and braids, I instantly recognized my middle school self the first day I'd met Bruce.

"That is so cool," she – *I* – squealed as she grabbed Bruce's bike. "Can I ride it?"

I smiled. I remembered the first day I tried the bike, Bruce running beside me as I raced down our street, the wind in my face, my eyes closed as I enjoyed the feeling of flying. We had spent the entire day together. The first of many days together.

I felt a small ache on the right side of my knee, and I looked down to see something glowing there, a reminder of a day Bruce and I had snuck out after dark and had tried to ride the bike down the hill behind our houses. I'd fallen, I remembered, scraping my knee against a rock, the blood coming from the wound scaring both of us, but not enough to run home and face our parents. Bruce had tried to stop the bleeding as best as he could, and I'd done everything I could not to scream bloody murder.

I smiled. We'd been so innocent then, the only worries in our lives being what our parents would do if they caught us outside when we weren't supposed to be.

"You should get one," child-Bruce told the little girl by his side. "Then we can race!"

I grinned.

"Grow up, Bruce!"

I almost laughed as I heard the snarky tone that was my go-to voice for the first two years of high school. I saw the teenager I'd been then, my long hair tied back in a ponytail, kicking at Bruce as he tried to shoot at me with a water gun.

"Come on, Honor!" he teased. "Show me what you're made of."

I remembered how much I'd held back from hurting Bruce that day, my feelings for him mixed and perplexing. The boy who was sometimes charming and sometimes a complete ass. I'd fallen for him hard even though we'd both agreed to keep things casual for a while – so what we had didn't go against his "one-month policy."

"One girl for one month," Bruce had told me once. "That's all the energy I have."

I'd hated that about him, how he made me feel special while at the same time assuring me that he had no intentions of making something long-term work.

Then he'd made it official on my sixteenth birthday, moving us from a casual friendship to an exclusive couple.

Except now I wondered how much of his original attitude had always been beneath the surface, hovering in the background. How much of it was still there.

The teenagers disappeared, disintegrating in the same cloud of smoke that had taken him before, and for a few minutes, I was surrounded by nothing but darkness. I floated about uneasily, my eyes waiting for the next set of images, memories to fill in the blankness about me. I felt pressure on my shoulders again, as if someone was trying to shake me awake, and I shook it off. In the distance, I heard gunfire, loud and threatening, and a shiver ran through me. Something exploded farther away, and suddenly I felt hands grab me by the arms, pulling at me, my body moving through the empty space around me as if on their own.

"We need to find shelter," I heard a man's voice say, and I quickly looked about to locate the source of the voice.

To my right, something flickered into view, hazy at first, a figure I couldn't recognize. A man. I squinted for a better look, but he quickly disappeared as the hands on my arms loosened.

I was floating again.

"Go slow."

My voice this time.

I watched as my bedroom assembled itself around me. I watched the teenager in my bed, under the covers, with Bruce on top of me. I remembered that night clearly, the first time we'd slept together, a week before senior prom. My parents had been visiting my aunt in Connecticut, and Bruce had come over to spend the night.

Despite the awkwardness, despite the initial pain, it had been a good night. Many of my friends told me that the first time was never good, but my first time had been okay. The touch of his hand, the heat between us, the way his lips had caressed me. For the first time since we'd become a couple, I felt a true connection between the two of us. It made the wrong between us better.

"Marry me."

He'd proposed the next morning, two high school kids sitting at the kitchen table in our underwear, sipping coffee as we smiled at each other. It had been a strange proposal, sudden, out of the blue, and we'd laughed it off as us being too young, but Bruce had continued to make comments about our future as if it'd been set. When he proposed for real a little over a year later, I'd accepted without a second thought.

My father had been against it, voicing his opinion about Bruce loud and clear – sometimes in front of Bruce – but eventually, I'd made him come around enough to at least be civil to my fiancé.

Not that I would've changed my mind. I could be stubborn when it suited me.

The scene from my past disintegrated, and I was left alone again with my thoughts, floating in my endless nothingness, wondering when it would end. There was more gunfire, another explosion, but this time, no hands pulled me.

Without warning, the darkness around me begin to dissipate, replaced with bright colors of white and blue and yellow. I saw images I couldn't make out, flashing quickly, randomly, appearing and disappearing just as fast.

An old woman with grandchildren sitting in a circle around her as they smiled at her.

A man walked into a hospital room, and my heart fluttered.

Bruce standing by my side, his smile sad, his face aged.

The images became sensations. Sounds.

Someone held my hand and squeezed.

A sweet and gentle kiss.

A soft and loving touch.

A hug.

A scream.

A baby's cry.

A child's laugh.

It was all so sudden, so overwhelming that I could barely breathe.

The hands were on my shoulders again, pulling, this time, more desperately, and I lashed out. Hands grabbed my wrists and pinned my arms down. Someone hissed at me to calm down. I tried to move again, and the hands tightened.

I was being shoved, as if a force had taken my entire body and was pushing it toward something. I felt the friction of the air against my body as the force picked up speed, and then suddenly, it was like I was being catapulted through the darkness, unable to stop myself. I opened my mouth to scream, but nothing came out. Then, just as quickly as it started, it stopped.

I opened my eyes.

Chapter 4

There's this place between sleep and fully awake where, as a child, I'd often found myself lost, my mind trying to decide whether it should come into focus or just slip back into slumber. I hadn't felt that feeling in a long time. Morning in the military didn't allow for that sort of reflection.

I felt it now though.

It took me a few minutes, long minutes that I relished in, but soon my mind made its decision and decided waking up was the best option. A part of me felt cheated out of some much needed rest, but I opened my eyes regardless.

When the world finally came into focus, the first thing I registered were the stars. There were millions of them shining in the sky above me, a tapestry of little lights that looked like a large connect-the-dots picture that was begging to be drawn. I'd never seen this many before, not even in the desert.

I remembered a time when my father had taken me and Ennis stargazing, something about being able to find our way if we ever got lost. I hadn't paid much attention then, being more concerned with the upcoming junior dance than I was with stars. I found myself wishing I'd paid better attention, because what

I was seeing not only amazed me but brought back childhood memories that seemed a little incomplete.

"One day, Honor," my father had said, *"these little dots in the sky might be your salvation."*

He was always saying things like that, my father, and I had always scoffed at it. He was a philosophical man, a part about his personality I'd never understood, especially with the military background. My mother said it was that part of him that had helped her see past the chiseled personality and no-bullshit attitude he usually carried around.

I loved the man, but to me, he would always be Peter Daviot, ex-army, the man who still scared the shit out of Bruce. After what Bruce had just pulled, maybe he deserved to be scared.

I blinked a few times as my eyes watered, the soft breeze around me picking up, brushing some hair into my eyes. My neck clench when I tried to move it, the sharp pain shooting upwards and giving me an instant headache that made me groan. I felt the back of my head, my hand pressing softly on a bump there that pulsated at my touch. I winced, hoping the nasty thing didn't mean I had a concussion.

In an instant, it all came back to me. The drive down the highway, the sound of the Chelsea River, the accident, the skidding, the crashing. Images of it all flashed through my mind, and for several seconds, I panicked. I felt around me, my hands touching soft grass, wet with the night's dew...and then I wondered where everyone was.

There were no sirens nearby, no screaming or shouting, no hands on my head or under my body, trying to carry me to safety. It was like I'd been thrown out of the car and had landed where no one was looking. Was I thrown out of the car? I couldn't remember.

I tried to push myself up, but the headache mixed with dizziness and the world around me spun out of control. I closed my eyes and tried desperately to fight the vertigo as I laid back down, wondering just how much damage the accident had done. The bump on my head was definitely enough to make me think twice about immediately inspecting the rest of my body.

My mind went back to the accident, how the truck had slammed into my car, how I'd felt my car do somersaults before stopping dead. It was a miracle I was alive, really, but it still bothered me that I was lying out in the open with no help. I didn't remember being thrown, but it was the only thing that made sense. Except I couldn't hear any sirens or anything else for that matter. It was like the world had forgotten about me.

A muffled gunshot made my eyes snap open, and I was back in Iraq. I sat up immediately, ready for the worst. My entire body screamed in protest. My head, angered at the sudden movement, felt like I'd taken a jackhammer to my skull. No matter what happened with the car, my body was warning me that I was in no way ready to face whatever it was I was getting ready to face. But, the adrenaline had kicked in, and the pain was slowly fading into the more manageable background.

I got up slowly, pushing first onto my knees before I attempted to stand straight. Severe pain shot through my leg, and I quickly found myself on the ground again, the fire in my ankle scorching as I shut my eyes in frustration.

Dammit!

"I am quite surprised you are able to stand."

My head snapped around as I realized for the first time that I wasn't alone.

I couldn't see him clearly, and it was definitely a him. The voice was masculine, with a hint of some sort of accent I didn't recognize. It was dark despite the starlight, and the corner he sat in threw shadows across him that made it impossible for me to discern any features.

He shifted, one leg moving over the other as the coat he wore seemed to flutter about him. A hat covered his head, broad-brimmed and rolled up on one side. What looked like a cane protruded from under his coat, and I could see the tops of a pair of strange-looking boots.

He looked like he had been on his way to a costume party.

I rolled over so that I sat up in front of him, my eyes squinting as I tried to get a good look at him. He cocked his head and pointed at me.

"Quite an unusual choice of attire," he said. "Where are you from?"

The accent was some kind of British and would have been exotically appealing if I hadn't started to feel the adrenaline ebb and the pain return.

"Are you the one on guard duty?" I asked, my voice so raspy I barely recognized myself. I wondered if he had volunteered to stay with me until the medics arrived. Maybe they hadn't wanted to move me just yet. Maybe I'd rolled down an embankment. My brain was still trying to make sense of it all.

"No," he said, sounding amused. "I am simply waiting until morning."

I frowned and coughed, my throat burning as I tried to speak. "Out here?"

"The safest place for now."

Great, I thought. They left me with a complete lunatic.

I tried to get up again and groaned in pain, my

ankle letting me know that moving about was not a good idea. I winced as I dragged myself to a nearby tree and leaned my head against the bark. I looked about, trying to discern which way the highway was but couldn't see anything in the dark. Where were the lights?

"You seem lost."

I fought the urge to say something snarky in response.

"Do you need anything to drink?" he asked.

I hadn't thought about it until he mentioned it, and I suddenly noticed that I was parched. I nodded, not trusting my voice again.

He stood slowly, then walked out into the dim light of the stars, allowing me to get a better look at him. Damn, he was good-looking. Dark waves brushed his shoulders as he handed me his flask, and I found myself staring into a pair of intelligent eyes whose color was undetectable in the darkness. He frowned at me, a look that was less than friendly, and I wondered how long he had been sitting there, waiting for me to wake up.

The man was definitely dressed for some sort of event, his overcoat falling well below the knees, two rows of buttons down the front, the lapels lying loose and barely hiding the breast coat labels below. He wore a pair of breeches over stockings that went up to his knees, the side buckles the loudest sound in the darkness.

I took a drink from the flask, instantly spitting it out when the strong taste hit my tongue. I'd never tasted anything like it.

"I don't have a lot of that," he said, sitting down again. "I would prefer to save a bit for the remainder of the night."

I took another drink, winced as I swallowed, and then closed the flask again. I looked down as I felt something rough against the pads of my fingers. The initials carved into it were easy to read, even in the dim light.

"GL?" I rasped out.

"Gracen Lightwood," he explained.

I wondered if the accent was real. I knew there were nuances to British accents that specified where people were from, but I'd never been able to tell the difference.

"And you?" he asked.

"Daviot," I replied and began to cough again. My throat hurt like a bitch.

"That sounds French," Gracen said.

I shrugged. "American, born and raised."

"Born and raised?" He repeated the phrase back to me like he'd never heard it before.

Okay, maybe he wasn't as smart as I first thought.

"I was a military brat for the first few years of my life, so I was all over before my father decided to move us out to the suburbs after he retired," I managed to say. "What about you?"

He was quiet for a minute, then leaned forward, his elbows resting near his breeches buckles as he tipped his hat up a bit.

"Is this how all natural born colonists speak?"

Wow, he was really going all out for this role.

I looked around me again, my eyes adjusting to the dark, the terrain unfamiliar to me. In the distance, I heard more gunfire, a few shots that echoed across the night sky, but there was something strange about them I couldn't quite place. I squinted and tried to make out where the highway was, but couldn't see anything.

"Where are we?" I asked, starting to get nervous.

"We are outside Boston," he said. "I found you lying a bit off that way," he pointed East, "in a most peculiar fashion, I might add. You took me quite by surprise."

I frowned. So he wasn't babysitting me after all. Apparently, no one even knew I was here. A flash of fear went through me. I could handle myself, and I wasn't a small woman, but I estimated him to be at least six-four. And I was injured.

"Where's the highway?" I asked, perking my ears, hoping to hear the sounds of distant vehicles, something to give me an idea of where I was and how I could get away from the man sitting across from me.

"The highway?"

"Yes, the highway," I said, my tone sharpening before another coughing fit silenced me for a moment. "I was in an accident, and I was probably thrown out of my car. I need to get back there."

He was staring at me now like I was the one with a few screws loose.

"Oh, come on, drop the gimmick already, would you," I rasped. "I'm beat up pretty bad, and I probably need medical attention."

"I did not see any blood, nor did any limbs appear broken," he said. "Aside from your ankle, I am sure you are in fine health."

"Really?" I didn't bother to hide my skepticism.

"Before I pulled you here, I ensured nothing was broken."

"You pulled me here?"

"I could not leave you out in the field like that, could I?"

"What field?"

"For God's sake, man, calm down," he snapped. "Keep your voice down."

That was the last thing I wanted to do. I wanted to scream at the top of my lungs. No matter how friendly he appeared to be, something was off here. The hairs on the back of my neck, on my arms, were standing up. Electricity zinged across my nerves, crackled in the air.

"I appreciate your help, but if you'll just point me to the EMTs, they'll take care of me from here."

"I can barely make sense of anything you are saying." His voice was tinged with annoyance. "And quite honestly, your level of gratefulness borders on rudeness."

I was being rude?

"Like I said, thanks for what you did, but I need to get home. My father's probably worried sick, and I don't even have my phone on me to call him. So, if you don't mind, just point me in the right direction, and I'll find a way to wobble over."

Gracen chuckled softly, and I wondered if I'd run into some sort of serial killer.

"You are a quite amusing, young man," he said. "I am quite unfamiliar to the linguistics of what you are saying, but I assure you, if your father is worried about you, being outside Boston right now is probably best."

I hesitated, briefly wondering if I should be insulted that he was mistaking me for a man. My hair was down to my chin, but Gracen's hair was about the same length. While he had raven-black waves, mine was a rich chestnut brown. I'd been told I had unique eyes, an almost silvery gray color, and I'd always thought of myself as relatively attractive. Him mistaking me for a man put a bit of a hole in that belief, though, I supposed, my features were more androgynous than feminine, especially with all the dirt and sweat on my face. And my hoarse voice. I decided I'd take it. If this guy was some sort of serial killer, I didn't want to give him any new ideas.

A soft breeze picked up and blew into my clothes, causing me to shiver. I pulled up my legs and pressed my knees to my chest, wrapping my arms around them as I tried to stop the cold from doing more. He stood up and walked over, taking off his overcoat and handing it to me.

"It's quite a surprise you hadn't frozen to death out there," he said, "what with the clothes you're wearing. The fashion is new to me."

"How about you help me up, and we find somewhere warmer?" I asked.

"I told you, we're safer here," he said.

The hair on my neck prickled again. "From what?"

"I could light a fire, but that would draw attention to us, and we don't want that kind of attention." He ignored my question. Sort of. "Not now. Not here."

"What does that even mean?" I asked, incredibly annoyed.

"When was the last time you were in Boston?" he asked, frowning at me like I was from another planet.

"Six months ago," I whispered.

He nodded, as if what I said cleared a few things up for him. "I think I understand better now. You must not have heard. The city has been under siege since April."

Chapter 5

When I finally found my voice, sort of, I asked what probably seemed like the most inane question ever. "What siege?"

Whatever game he was playing, I didn't feel like playing along anymore. For someone who'd served in the military, joking about things like sieges wasn't funny.

But still...there were those gunshots I heard.

Something was going on, and I needed to find out what it was. I was proud to serve my country, but my family was still my first priority. If they were in danger, I needed to understand the enemy.

At this point, though, I wasn't sure if the enemy was out there somewhere, or here, sitting across from me.

"The English," Gracen said. "They arrived in early April. The city's been under siege since then."

"What are you talking about?" I asked. "The British are our allies. Why would they attack us?"

He stood up and stretched, obviously impatient with my questions. "While the siege of Boston may perhaps be news, I can't imagine that there's a corner of the colonies that isn't aware of the rebellion." He gave me a hard look. "Things will only get worse if you ask me. They named George Washington Commander in Chief. After Lexington and Concord, things will probably just get bloodier."

The words threw me back in time...or was it forward?

I was suddenly at home again, a high school teenager too bored to do anything useful with her time. Bruce had gone to Virginia Beach on spring break with a couple of his cousins. He'd blown off my concerns, but that didn't stop me from worrying about what he'd do when I wasn't around to remind him that he had a girlfriend. I hadn't made too big of a deal about it though. I didn't want him to think that I didn't trust him.

Still, I needed to get my mind off of things, and the only way to do that was fill my time with something useful.

The only problem was, I had no idea what.

I walked into my brother's room. Ennis was resting his head on the palms of his hands, textbooks open around him as he studied for his upcoming finals. I strode in like I owned the place and plopped down on the bed, sighing loud enough to get his attention.

"Not now, Honor," Ennis said, flipping a page as he compared one text to the other.

"I'm bored," I whined, grabbing one of the many texts that were strewn all over his bed. "Give me something to do."

"Honor, seriously, I have work to do." His irritation was clear in his voice, but I didn't pay any attention to it.

It was an older brother's job to be annoyed by his little sister.

"What is this stuff, anyway?"

"It's called history, Honor. Maybe you should think about checking it out sometime. You know what they say about people who don't learn from it."

I scowled at him as I stood up and walked over to his desk. I peered over his shoulder. He had notes scribbled everywhere, the textbooks in front of him taking up half his working space. I squinted as I tried to read the small print, then quickly gave up. He wasn't wrong about my dislike of history. What the hell kind of major was that anyway? What did someone do with a history degree besides teach?

I knew for a fact that Dad felt the same way. The only reason he'd agreed to pay for a year of college before Ennis enlisted was because he hoped my brother would figure out the futility of what he was doing.

So far, it hadn't worked.

"If you want to make yourself useful, you can summarize this," Ennis said, pushing one of the textbooks aside and pointing at a passage he'd highlighted. "You do know how to do that, right?"

I glared at him. I wanted to be a pediatrician, and I had the grades to support my ambition. Math and science may have been my strong point, but I wasn't a complete idiot when it came to English.

Except, as I tried to wade through the dense prose I was supposed to be summarizing, I wondered if maybe I was an idiot. I barely got to the end of one sentence before I forgot the beginning of it.

"Too much?"

"Who the hell writes these things, anyway?" I snapped as I set the book back down in front of him.

He chuckled and sat back, rubbing his eyes. "So, all you'll ever know about American history is what you see on TV, huh?"

I shrugged. "Why bother? It's over and done with. The past is the past."

Ennis shook his head, wearing that condescending smile that drove me nuts. "That's not why we learn history, Honor."

"Enlighten me then, oh wise one."

"If we know what we did wrong before, we can prevent it from happening again."

I raised an eyebrow, a little skeptical. "And how have we been doing so far?"

"Terribly," he admitted and gave me a sideways glance. "Probably because not many of us care to read about the past."

I punched his shoulder before looking back down at the textbooks and frowning. "So, you think we'll stop making mistakes if we study all this stuff?"

He shrugged. "Maybe." He didn't sound too convinced. "Maybe we'll just understand the present and know how to better handle the future."

"Sorry, but I'm not buying it."

"Take this, for example," Ennis said, turning a few pages back to find what he was looking for. "The Battle of Bunker Hill. The English charged up Breed's Hill on June 17th, 1775 and defeated the colonial army there. In the process, they suffered so much loss that their initial plan of breaking out of Boston was lost. The battle resulted in a stalemate, but the fact that the colonial army had stood up to the British was enough to motivate Washington and keep the Revolution going."

I frowned and shook my head. "We lost," I said. "How was that a motivator?"

Ennis sighed and shook his head. "One day you'll realize that numbers don't matter, and sometimes even a win or loss of a battle doesn't matter. A small loss can be seen as a major victory if you look at the grand scheme of things. I guess maybe that's what I mean by learning from history. It's the ability to see the big picture."

I looked at Ennis, still skeptical, but I didn't want to ask for clarification. I didn't think he'd talk down to me, but I was pretty sure he'd bore me to death. He saw the look on my face and pushed at me, laughing as he did it. Closing the text book he'd read from, he tossed it at me.

"Read, Honor," he said. "It might just save your life one day."

"You don't need this?" I asked, wondering just how much time it would kill.

"Not now," he said. "Give it to me after you've had a chance to learn something that isn't about numbers and theorems."

I read several chapters, I remembered, and had been pleasantly surprised by how interesting it had been when I looked at it the way Ennis had. If he did end up going into education, his students would be lucky to have him.

I sat silently, staring at Gracen as he walked around in small circles. This had to be some sort of mistake. A Revolutionary War re-enactment actor who hit his head during the accident.

Except it didn't explain the lack of city lights. The absence of my car and the highway. Before I could second guess myself, I forced the question I didn't want to consider.

"What's today's date?"

He thought a moment before he answered. "June sixteenth."

That, at least, was right, but the sinking feeling in the pit of my stomach made me ask for clarification. "What year?"

He crouched down in front of me, his gaze fixing on me in a way that made me want to squirm. "That is an odd question to ask."

"What year is it?" I asked again, unwilling to get into any unneeded arguments.

"I had heard that education in some parts of the colonies was lacking, but I hadn't realized how much so."

I glared at him and ignored the insult. "The year," I demanded.

He hesitated, eyeing me closely, as if he wasn't sure if he should be worried about me. "Seventeen seventy-five," he finally said.

All the air left my lungs, and I leaned back.

Fuck me.

What the *hell* happened?

Chapter 6

I remember the first time I truly felt like I had no control over the world around me.

I'd been on my first tour, out on a reconnaissance mission that was supposed to go smoothly for a newbie medic like me. I'd been barely nineteen, freshly engaged, and still trying to wrap my head around where I was. I believed in what I was doing, and growing up in a military family, was aware of the risks.

Knowing something and then *knowing* it, however, were two totally different things.

Needless to say, my unit had been attacked in an area that we'd thought was safe. None of us had been prepared for the assault, and we'd lost two soldiers before I'd even had a chance to get to them.

It was my first time witnessing death firsthand, deaths that I knew weren't my fault, but that I still blamed myself for. Logically, I knew that if I would've gone after them, I'd most likely have been killed too, and even if I hadn't, I most likely couldn't have saved them anyway. It hadn't taken away my guilt though. I told myself that there was nothing I could've done, that the entire thing had been completely out of my control, and a part of me knew it, remembered how the chaos had felt.

That was one of those moments that had forever altered my way of thinking, my way of seeing the world, and I knew it wasn't only due to the deaths, but rather the stark realization that I had no control over any of it.

This was another of those times.

I leaned back against the tree, my mind caught in an endless spin as it tried to make sense of my situation. A part of me still wanted to believe that it was all a show, the figments of a mad man's imagination. He was tricking me. It had to be that. It couldn't be anything else.

But it wasn't like I could actually prove him wrong. My ankle made it almost impossible to get up on my own, and at the moment, I wasn't even sure if it would help. If Gracen was as deranged as I knew he must be to expect me to believe his story, he would be on me before I managed to get more than a few steps. And based on what I'd seen, there wasn't anyone around who'd hear me if I yelled for help.

I looked over at him as he lay on the ground in the protection of the brush, his hat cocked over his eyes as he snored. He'd fallen asleep for about an hour before but had already woken twice at the slightest sounds. Between my ankle and not knowing the terrain, I had little hope of being quiet enough to escape without him knowing it.

I rested my head against the tree behind me, weighing my options. I knew my training would be next to useless with my ankle, unless he was stupid enough to come too close. It was the cane that worried me. It was a weapon that could be an issue if he was willing to use it. At that moment, I wished I'd revealed to him that I was a woman. Men had a habit of underestimating women, so if I tried to do something, he would probably try and grab me instead of using the cane. That would put me at an advantage.

I watched him turn over, and when the next couple gunshots fired without waking him, I knew this was my most likely opportunity. I rolled over slowly, the twigs under me snapping as I moved. I kept my eyes locked on his back, seeing if the sounds would wake him. I remembered how my father could sleep through a marching band, just to wake up at the sound of my brother's cough from across the hall.

I prayed Gracen wasn't similarly tuned to breaking twigs.

When he still didn't move, I risked pushing myself up, placing most of my weight on my good leg as I used the tree for support. The pain in my bad ankle had subsided, but I decided against trying to see how much I could use it. With any luck, I could get far enough without testing it too much, and, by morning, I'd be far from here, and the swelling would have gone down.

I started to move in short hops, looking back once or twice to see if he'd woken up, but his back was still to me, and it didn't seem like that was going to change. Feeling bolder, I quickened my pace, quickly pushing through the trees until I found myself on an open plain.

That was when I realized that Gracen wasn't crazy after all.

There was no highway. There were no flashing lights from distant ambulances or the honking of cars. There were no towering buildings in the distance or the familiar Boston lights shining back at me. As far as I could see, the city I knew didn't exist.

I could see Boston, but it was nothing like the Boston I knew.

Gunshots blasted again, and I finally realized what was weird about them. They weren't the gunfire I'd become accustomed to in the army. Those weren't modern guns. Even if there was some sort of rational reason for why I kept hearing shooting from Boston, I could think of no reason as to why they'd be using old-fashioned guns.

I didn't know how or why it had happened. I had no explanation for any of it, but it didn't matter.

I was in the past. In 1775 Colonial America, to be specific.

I tried to remember what I'd read in my brother's book and realized that walking towards Boston would either get me killed or worse. The battle would be across the river, but still too close for comfort. Even if the British soldiers assumed that I was a man, I doubted they'd be inclined to be compassionate to someone sneaking around the night before a battle.

Even though I now knew that Gracen was telling the truth about where – *when* – I was, he was still a stranger, and I didn't know where his loyalties lay.

I did, however, know that I'd feel more comfortable with colonists than I would with the Brits. I didn't know where the army was, but I figured I would have better luck finding a "rebel" colonist out there somewhere than trying to sneak past the British army in Boston. My ankle was slowing me down, but I didn't stop moving. I needed to get as far away from here as possible, especially since I knew exactly what was going to happen tomorrow.

I found a road, keeping to the tree-line as I followed it, ready to hide if anything seemed out of the ordinary. My training was starting to kick in, my senses more alert, the darkness around me slowly becoming more comforting. I tried to make as little noise as possible, stopping as often as I needed to rest in the hopes that I wouldn't collapse from fatigue. The truth was, I didn't know half the extent of my injuries, and I had a feeling that my ankle was the least of my worries. The knot on my head throbbed in time with my pulse, which wasn't exactly comforting.

I heard the sounds of footsteps ahead, and I quickly pushed deeper into the woods. I crouched down, making sure to keep my weight off my bad ankle, and watched the road. I listened closely, and soon, the sounds of men came closer. A few minutes later, they appeared, their coats brown, their muskets held against their shoulders as they patrolled down the road.

Brown coats, not red ones.

Colonials.

This was my chance to get with people I'd be able to trust. I pushed myself to my feet, but just before I could make my presence known, something hard hit the back of my head.

My knees buckled as the world around me started to go dark, and the last thing I knew before I passed out was that a pair of arms kept me from going to the ground.

I came to with a deep, excruciating pain in the back of my head that made everything else I was feeling in my body seem like mild aches.

My vision swam in and out of focus, and when I was finally able to blink the world back into proper view, Gracen was sitting a few feet away from me looking like he'd just been to hell and back. His hat was missing, his hair in wild disarray. His overcoat was draped over his shoulders like a cape, and he was holding his cane in both hands.

I tried to move, and it was only when I couldn't that I realized my hands had been tied together behind my back. The ropes dug into my skin, and I had a feeling that even if I were able to break free, the numbness would render them useless for a while.

I glared at him, but he merely raised an eyebrow in response.

"Untie my hands," I demanded.

His grip on his cane tightened even as his frown deepened. "Do you have any idea what you could have done?"

"I have a pretty good idea, actually," I hissed. "I'm not as stupid as you seem to think I am."

"You almost got us both killed," he hissed back. "You're a sympathizer, aren't you? Or is it more than that? Are you a spy? A soldier?"

"None of the above," I said. And it was true. Technically. The army I was a soldier in didn't actually exist yet. "I just needed to get away from Boston."

"Why?" Gracen asked. Then, before I could decide whether or not to answer, he spoke again, "On second thought, don't answer that. I can't risk being seen with you. My family can't be tied to sympathizers."

I struggled against the ropes, stopping only as they dug deeper into my skin. There was no way around it. If I wanted to leave, I'd have to talk my way out of this.

"Listen, I'm grateful for what you've done," I started, "but I can't be here. I need to get home. There's no reason for me to be here."

He shook his head. "I can't let you go now. It's too dangerous, and since I'm the only one of us who seems to understand how much, you're staying put until dawn."

I regarded him carefully, weighing my options and quickly realized that I didn't actually have any. "What then?" I asked.

"Then you will be free to go," he said. "You shall go your way, and I shall go mine."

I wanted to tell him that dawn would be a little bit too late, that the gunfire we were still hearing wouldn't stop but would become louder, closer. That by the time the sun came up tomorrow, things would get much more complicated.

But I kept my mouth shut, unwilling to risk giving away who I really was and the time I was actually from. Besides, I doubted he'd believe me. I didn't believe it myself, and I was living it.

"So we wait?" I asked.

He nodded and sat back, his eyes fixed on me as he tried to find a comfortable position. I tried to do the same, but my hands made that an impossibility. Between that and the insanity of the last few hours, I doubted I'd get any sleep. From the way Gracen was looking at me, it was a fair bet he wouldn't be sleeping either.

It was going to be a long night.

Chapter 7

My father was a large man, the kind who made you think twice before you decided to do anything stupid. His size had kept him out of trouble for most of his life, and the scowl he usually kept plastered on his face had pretty much the same effect. A military man to the core, a patriot at heart, he exemplified everything the US Army stood for.

And he scared the shit out of pretty much everyone who saw him.

But I knew the real him. I knew the heart of gold he concealed, the warm hugs he gave, the smiles that came when he was proud. There were times when I felt like he had ruined my future forever, that no other man could ever match up to him.

Maybe that was why I put up with so much of Bruce's shit, because on some level, I felt like my expectations were too high.

I also knew that if my father found out some of the shit Bruce pulled, my fiancé would've come face-to-face with the scariest my father could be.

Which was what happened one night I came home crying after Bruce and I had been in a terrible fight.

I'd just returned from my first tour and had a week of leave. I'd gone home but had spent my first night on a date with Bruce...where he'd proceeded to drink too much and make snide comments about how women looked in uniform. When I called him on it, he'd gone into a fifteen-minute tirade about how things hadn't been easy for him while I was gone. How hard it'd been to go that long without seeing me. Without sex.

That was the last straw. I'd stormed out and taken a cab home. Dad hadn't said a word. Hadn't asked me what was wrong. He'd just held me until I stopped crying.

I hadn't heard him leave later that night, but the next day, Bruce had come to apologize. The moment I saw his expression when my dad came down the stairs behind me, I'd known why Bruce had come.

I wondered what my father would've thought of Gracen. Somehow, I didn't get the impression that he would be as easily intimidated as Bruce. Dad would've liked that.

I, however, wasn't so sure I liked it. Or him, for that matter.

As the night dragged on, sleep didn't get any closer. I tossed and turned, my hands hurting more and more as the ropes rubbed my skin raw. While I was used to not being in the most comfortable places to sleep, this was definitely on the top of my discomfort list.

Finally, I gave up and looked over to where Gracen sat. His eyes were closed, his cane still in his grasp.

I had to admit he was a handsome man, despite his crude ways of dealing with situations. His high cheekbones and chiseled jaw made him easy on the eyes, and his tousled hair just added to the charm. The fact that he wasn't wearing a wig, like a lot of people during this time period, told me that he was as pretentious as his accent made him sound.

If I'd met him in another place and time, I would have probably given him more than just a second glance. He was the kind of man who commanded attention, of that much I was sure.

My mind wandered back to Bruce, and I wondered what he was doing now or if my parents had called him when I didn't arrive home. Then again, even if they had, there was no guarantee he would've answered. I doubted he'd be calling me again anytime soon to try to get me to come early. He might've sounded annoyed at first, but I didn't doubt he'd find a way to get over it. Over the years, he'd lost the part of him that had always put me first – if he'd ever really had it to begin with.

I wondered what would have happened if I'd done as he asked and gotten straight on a plane to Vegas. My parents would've been upset, my father probably even more than my mother. I knew he'd been looking forward to my return and had wanted to discuss my possible re-enlistment before I made a final decision. I was surprised when he supported my decision to eventually open my own pediatric practice, even suggesting that he could lease a small space downtown to help me set up. When I first mentioned that this might be the time to make that change, I thought he'd give me hell for wanting out, but he hadn't.

He was probably going out of his mind by now and trying not to show it. My mother would definitely be worried sick. I could only imagine how Ennis was handling it. I wished there was some way for me to let them know that I was okay.

If being tied up in the company of an eighteenth-century Loyalist a day before one of the precursor battles of the American Revolution was any indication of me being okay.

I closed my eyes and tried to fall asleep, but my mind was still racing from worry, from all of the new information. How the hell was this even possible? How had I gotten here?

I retraced everything that I could remember. The accident, the man trying to unbuckle me from the car, everything, but I still couldn't find any logical explanation for the time warp I'd found myself in. I vaguely remembered my time in the darkness, the feeling of being hurled back and forth, the arms that had grabbed and pulled me. My mind tried hard to piece things together. It still didn't make any sense, and I was slowly starting to realize that there might not ever be an answer.

I might just have to accept that I was in 1775...and might never get back to my own time.

I wasn't sure if I could, but I was too tired to do anything about it now, even if the ropes around my wrists had left me with any viable options. I coughed and shook my head, trying to work out the knots in my neck and fight the pair of throbbing spots on the back of my skull. One from the accident, the other from Gracen.

"If you plan to stay awake all night, do you mind keeping it down," he spoke up without opening his eyes.

I looked at him and grinned. If I had to be miserable, at least I knew he wasn't doing much better. "I doubt my coughing is what's keeping you awake," I said.

He opened his eyes and glared at me. "It wouldn't, if you'd bloody lie down and go to sleep."

I used my best sarcastic voice. "I'm sorry if the prisoner is causing you problems."

"You're not a prisoner."

I turned slightly to my side to show him the ropes, an eyebrow raised as I dared him to contradict the obvious.

"Well, at least not for long," he amended. "Believe me, I want to get rid of you as much as you wish to be rid of me, but I cannot have you going off to the rebels."

"Why do you even care?" I asked. "If I truly were a sympathizer, wouldn't the best option be to send me over to the colonists?"

His eyes widened as he leaned forward, all pretense of sleep gone. "Are you bloody mad, man?" He sounded shocked. "Let you tell them that Gracen Lightwood pulled you from the fields where the army would have certainly found you, most likely held you as a spy? Do you know what that would do to my family?"

I rolled my eyes. "There's no need to get overdramatic."

He scowled at me. "You know nothing of my family, Mr. Daviot. My father, Roston Lightwood, supports the English position here in the colonies more than he's supported me. His wealth depends on the British, and he would rather his family die before ever having any of us associated with the rebels."

"That's a shame," I muttered, knowing well what would happen to the Loyalists in the years to come.

"A shame?" Gracen asked in exasperation. "Bloody ungrateful, if you ask me."

"So you share your father's opinions?" I found myself honestly curious, not only making conversation.

"I have taken no side," he said. "This isn't my fight."

"You live here, don't you?"

"I was born in London."

Nice deflection. "That wasn't my question."

He looked down and used the tip of his cane to draw patterns in the dirt. "My father loves the Crown. He spent most of his life in service of the king. All he ever had was his work, and he was rewarded for it. It's why he brought us to the colonies. Shortly after I was born, he was given a tract of land just outside Boston for his services. Had he stayed in England, his inheritance would have been a pittance."

I was beginning to understand. "You feel the need to be just as grateful as your father."

He thought about it for a moment. "I suppose that is some of it. But I am a British citizen by birth, no matter where I make my home."

In a flash of memory, I remembered something I'd seen in some movie. How the people who were born and raised in England didn't consider the colonists to be British citizens...until it came to their blind obedience.

"You know that not everyone in the colonies enjoys the same liberties as British citizens, right?" I asked. "That the *rebels*, as you call them, just want to be treated equally."

He gave me a hard look. "The world is rarely so simple; something you colonists don't seem to understand."

I wanted to disagree. I did understand it. I had seen war. I had seen death. I'd seen what it meant to fight for what you believed in against people whose beliefs were just as strong. There was rarely any right side, rarely a winning side, and things were never clear cut or easy. No matter how righteous the cause, innocents were always in the line of fire.

But some things were worth fighting for, and I knew this had been one of them. America wasn't perfect, but I'd enlisted because I believed in my country.

"I think you should get some sleep," Gracen ended the conversation. "Sunrise will be in a couple hours, and if we're lucky, we can get away from here before the patrols make their rounds."

He stretched out on the ground this time, covered his face with his hat, and crossed his arms over his chest. I continued watching him until his breathing steadied, and a light snore escaped him. I didn't like him, I told myself, but I did wonder what would happen to him when the battle began tomorrow.

And what would happen to him as the rebellion became an official war? A war that the British would lose. I didn't know enough about British history to know how drastically the war affected their country, but I did know that it was a turning point that eventually led to America becoming one of the major world powers.

I reminded myself that none of it was my problem. That whatever happened to Gracen and his family had already happened long ago, just like the war had already taken place.

Sort of.

Trying to figure it all out made my head hurt even more.

I finally got into a relatively comfortable position, closed my eyes, and fell asleep.

Chapter 8

The cannon blast woke me even as I was being shaken.

The first thing I was aware of was the urgency with which Gracen was moving. Immediately on the heels of that thought was the change in the periodic gunfire I'd heard last night. It came faster now. Not as fast as it would in my time, but still enough of a change to remind me of where and when I was.

The Battle of Bunker Hill had begun.

"Did you know?" he asked as he cut the rope binding my hands. "Was this why you wanted to get away so urgently?"

"I had no idea," I lied, rubbing my sore wrists as I watched him throw a glance toward the city. In the light, he was even more handsome than the night before, his features clearer, his emerald eyes more piercing. The frown on his face, though, wasn't as appealing.

He looked at me as if I had tricked him somehow. "Did you attempt to keep me here?" he asked.

"Are you serious?" I asked incredulously. "I tried to get away from you. You were the one keeping me here against my will."

He pulled his overcoat on without taking his eyes

from the tree line. I knew what he was looking for, and I wanted to assure him that if we avoided Breed's Hill, we'd most likely pass by unseen. But I knew if I offered this bit of information, he'd want to know how I came by it, and that wasn't a story I could tell.

"I want nothing to do with this." Gracen's voice was hard. "You are free to do as you please, but I will not be a part of this madness."

I moved quickly to his side, pleased at how much better my ankle felt, and crouched beside him even as the sounds of muskets and cannons roared nearby. This was what I wanted to avoid last night, though, in hindsight, I realized it would have been a bad idea to join up with the soldiers now facing off against the British. While the British casualties would be more than double the American ones, it would still be a bloodbath.

"We should probably stick together," I said.

I'd told myself that Gracen wasn't my responsibility, but now that it came down to it, I couldn't leave him here, knowing what I did. Even though neither of us were soldiers in this war, it felt too much like leaving a man behind, no matter how things had originally played out for him.

He was moving now, and I followed. At least he was being cautious as he inched toward the river. As I walked behind him, I was unsure if I should give him details about where the majority of the fighting was taking place. My sense of direction was skewed at the moment, and I had no idea where we were in relation to Breed's Hill. Ennis would have known.

Keeping low and moving slow were our best bets. With neither of us being armed and me still limping a bit, I could only hope that if we ran into either side, they'd take us for civilians trying to avoid being shot.

Morning turned into afternoon as the heat rose

steadily. I wanted to ask Gracen how much farther, but being quiet was more important than the sweat pouring down my face. Theoretically, I'd known that Boston and the surrounding countryside would have looked different than what I was used to, but I hadn't realized how much. I was completely dependent on Gracen to lead me now. I was completely lost.

Then I saw the smoke.

Charlestown, Massachusetts was on fire.

Through the trees and brush, I could see flickers of orange and red. The people in Boston would have a better view. According to the book Ennis had given me to read, one of those Bostonians would be John Quincy Adams, a child now, but who would later become president.

The strange things we remember in moments of duress.

Even though the details were lost, the smell of the smoke and the sounds of battle drove home more than anything else just how great a price had been paid for our freedom. This was only one of many battles that would make up the war, and it wouldn't be long before the colonists would run out of bullets and resort to throwing rocks. It would be a bloodbath.

We had to leave before we were counted among the casualties.

I grabbed Gracen by the arm, but he wouldn't budge.

"My God," he whispered as he watched the flames across the Charles River.

I pulled harder. "Gracen, we have to move, now!"

He stumbled a few steps, his face pale. I didn't blame him. I'd seen war firsthand, and I felt sick to my stomach. For someone who'd never witnessed it, it was overwhelming. I pulled harder, and Gracen followed me a dozen feet or so before we were stopped by three muskets pointing straight at us.

"Halt, in the name of King George!"

Shit.

I pushed Gracen behind me, an involuntary act since there was no way I'd be able to protect either one of us, but I was also pretty sure he'd be useless if it came to a fight. The redcoat in the middle lowered his musket, coming toward us in slow strides. The other two kept their weapons trained right on us.

"Identify yourselves!" the leader demanded.

I held up my hands to show that I didn't have any weapons. Even though it irked me, I knew that we were safer with the British than the Americans at the moment.

"My name is Gracen Lightwood." He stepped around me, and I frowned at him. He ignored me. "I am the son of Roston Lightwood, a Loyalist to the Crown, and a friend to the British army."

The man looked at me, clearly expecting me to add my own identity to the mix. Gracen knew where my loyalties were, and I wasn't sure I could trust him to support any lies I might tell, but I also knew I couldn't tell the truth.

"Mr. Daviot is my steward," Gracen lied, putting a firm hand on my shoulder. "We were on our way to my estate when the fighting started, and we decided to take cover and wait out the battle."

The redcoat looked past us toward where the battle continued. He didn't even bother hiding his contempt at what I was sure he considered cowardly behavior. I had no doubt he wished to be with his comrades, charging the rebels on the hill. I wanted to tell him that he was better off here.

"In the name of King George, I am putting you under arrest and taking you to camp for questioning," the man said.

"Good man, I assure, there is no need–" Gracen began but immediately held his tongue when he was shot an angry glance. The other two soldiers came forward, clearly intending to do as they'd been told.

I couldn't let them take us to camp. I didn't know how close it was to Breed's Hill, for one thing. For another, I was somehow still passing as a man. If we were taken somewhere to be questioned, there was a good chance that my gender would be discovered which would cause more problems than I even wanted to think about.

Since I was unarmed, I needed to be fast. I said a quick prayer that my training back home would be as much of a surprise as my resistance and then moved. Kicking at the musket pointed at me, it fell to the side just as the man pulled the trigger. The sound of the shot was deafening, but it was the target I was worrying about, and the lead ball had the desired effect as it buried in one of the other soldier's legs.

As the musket was brought back around, the redcoat seemed eager to use the bayonet on me, but I grabbed the barrel and pulled it forward. I watched as the blade slid into the other soldier before he could do anything more than stare at us in shock.

The redcoat hit me, his fist slamming against the back of my head. I saw stars and staggered, pain shooting through my skull and down my spine. I let the adrenaline flood through me, giving me what I needed to move past the pain, and not a moment too soon. The soldier pulled his weapon out of his fallen comrade and turned it on me.

He thrust the bayonet toward me and the blade cut through my shirt and shoulder, drawing blood. It did little damage, and I ignored the pain as I pushed the weapon away and grabbed the soldier. My hands wrapped around his arm, and I brought his elbow upwards with tremendous force. The man screamed in pain as I felt his joint snap and the gun fell from his hand. He was quick though and managed a blow to the jaw that caught me enough off guard that I fell.

I was sure that would be it for me, but that was when Gracen moved. His cane caught the redcoat square in the jaw. The man staggered, surprised by the attack, but collected himself quickly. He went for Gracen, but I grabbed at him as he passed. His elbow connected with my temple, and my grip loosened enough for him to break free.

He grabbed his gun and turned on me, ignoring Gracen as the soldier who'd been shot joined in the fight. He grabbed Gracen's leg, but I barely had time to register it before the leader drove his bayonet down.

I screamed at the pain searing through my leg as the blade sliced through skin and muscle. Grabbing the barrel of the gun to keep the soldier from pulling the bayonet out, I kicked with my good leg. From the corner of my eye, I saw Gracen knocked to the ground. The man above me saw it too and reached for his dead comrade's gun.

Without thinking, I yanked the bayonet free, sending a fresh wave of pain blasting through my system. Swinging out, the bayonet sunk into the leader's side before he could reach Gracen. I twisted it sharply, and the soldier turned toward me. Our eyes locked for a brief second before he slumped to the ground.

I fell back, the pain in my leg and shoulder overcoming the adrenaline. A gunshot made me jump, and I looked over to see Gracen holding a small pistol, smoke still coming from the barrel. The injured soldier was now dead.

Gracen's eyes met mine, and I saw horror at what we'd done. I opened my mouth to tell him that we hadn't been given a choice, that it had been us or them, but I knew he wouldn't understand, not when he'd been so certain that his father's loyalties would protect him.

At the moment, however, that wasn't our biggest problem.

About thirty yards away, three more redcoats were running towards us, and I knew there was no getting away.

Chapter 9

"The key is to not get caught."

Wilkins and I had been doing grunt work all day, and all I wanted now was to grab a nap in the short time we had before dinner.

"Go to sleep, Wilkins," I called out.

"I'm serious, Daviot," he said. "This isn't a place where you want to play hero. To these people...anyone who's not Muslim is an infidel, and they're going to treat you like one. Probably worse since you're a woman doing a man's job."

I shook my head, knowing it was pointless to argue with his stereotyping. The truth was, I'd met several locals over the past couple months, most of whom had treated me with respect, some I even considered friends.

"When the going gets rough, Daviot, you run," Wilkins continued. "And if you can't run, you better make sure you have a bullet left that you can aim at your head."

I sat up on my elbow and looked over at him, frowning as he stared back at me with his child-like grin. "You know you're full of shit, right?"

"Am I?"

"Go to sleep!" This time, my tone was harsher, and when I laid back down, he didn't reply.

The water was cold, and I instantly snapped awake.

I was on my knees, my hands tied behind my back, and the wound on my leg crudely tied to stop the bleeding. My face and hair were dripping from the water they'd thrown on me.

I looked up from my kneeling position, taking in my surroundings. A few feet away from me sat Gracen. He was in a chair, frowning at the officer who leaned calmly against the edge of an oak table. I had a feeling Gracen had sold the same lie he'd given the other soldiers, which meant I was the more expendable of the two of us. The fact that the officer was smiling at me didn't make me feel any more at ease.

There were four other soldiers around us, and the closest one to me held the bucket that I assumed once contained the water that was now running down my face. I glanced at Gracen, my eyes catching his, and the worry I saw there was surprising.

"I always thought of you colonists as a rugged bunch, wild dogs running about and snapping your muzzles at anything that walked by." The officer sneered down at me. "While your friend put up a surprising fight, in the end, you were still no more than I expected."

I stared up at him, silent, unwilling to give him the satisfaction of a reply, though I knew exactly what he was talking about. The sound of gunfire had ceased, the battle obviously over. The British had won, but I knew what was coming. I gave the man a small smile.

"This amuses you?"

I nodded. "You might have won, but I'm pretty sure you've lost more than you've gained."

A fist connected with the side of my face, and I fell

backwards, unable to stop myself from hitting the ground hard. My cheek throbbed, but my leg hurt more. The way I'd fallen had pulled the muscles in my leg and made the wound bleed again.

"I do not like being here," the officer said, standing up and dusting his coat as he looked down at me. "I would much rather be home, among civilized people, but until this rebellion is quashed, I'm here. So, you will help me get home. Let us start with how many men are outside Boston, shall we?"

"I don't know," I answered.

A kick to my ribs and I gasped as the air was pushed from my lungs.

"When are your reinforcements arriving?"

I shook my head slowly. "I don't know."

Another kick, probably cracking my ribs.

The officer sighed heavily. "Lying will get you nowhere. Now, you know that someone such as yourself, dressed in non-regulation uniform, can be considered a spy. And we hang spies."

"I demand a meeting with General Gage," Gracen cut in.

The officer looked at him for a few seconds before back-handing him, the ring on his finger leaving a thin cut across his handsome cheek. "You don't make demands here."

"My name is Gracen Lightwood, captain." Gracen looked pissed. "My father is Roston Lightwood. We are loyal British subjects and friends to the Crown. Our lands were presented to us by the king himself. I demand to see General Gage."

The officer bent down, his face inches from Gracen's as he smiled. I'd seen that look before, and it wasn't one I cared to see now. This captain wouldn't be intimidated.

"I know your father," the captain said. "Now, I ask myself how he would react to knowing that his son was found in the company of a sympathizer, or worse, a colonist soldier. I doubt he'd be very pleased." The officer grabbed Gracen by the jaw. "He may ask to put the noose around your neck himself."

Gracen didn't even flinch. "Let us send for my father and see?"

The officer let go of Gracen and gave him a shove, knocking both Gracen and the chair onto the ground. One look at the expression in Gracen's eyes told me that no matter what his politics were coming in here, he wouldn't extend that loyalty to this captain.

"Now," the officer cut into my thoughts as he crouched in front of me, "let us discuss what information you will give me."

I shook my head and closed my eyes, bracing myself for another beating. When I felt pressure on my leg, a boot pressing down on my wound, my eyes snapped open, and I screamed in pain.

"This is bleeding badly," he said, his tone almost conversational. "You might not even make it to the gallows." He removed his foot and leaned closer. "Now, I can make all that pain go away, or I can make it much, much worse. The choice is yours."

I didn't answer, focusing instead on taking slow, deep breaths as I fought through the pain. I could take more, even though the prospect wasn't appealing. All I needed was for him to decide to leave me to die at some point and hope that I was able to escape.

Let them have their fun, for now. I planned to kill each and every one of them as soon as I had the chance.

The officer sighed and heavy hands grabbed me by the shoulders, picking me up. They dragged me to the opposite side of the tent and tossed me there to lick my wounds. The bucket was tossed aimlessly at me, the hard wood slamming against my head as it tumbled away. Dazed, I watched it roll...only to stop at the side of a musket, the protruding bayonet inches from where I lay.

I sat up slowly, exaggerating the extent of my pain as I watched the officer and soldiers shift their attention to Gracen. Two of them yanked him upright.

"You know, I do not consider colonists to be true British citizens," the officer said. "Not like you and I, Mr. Lightwood. I see them on the level of the Irish, or the Scots. A lower class of being. They can hardly be surprised to not be afforded the same liberties as those of us more deserving."

"I know what the colonies owe the Crown," Gracen said stiffly. "And as you pointed out, I am not colony born."

The officer nodded in mock approval, applauding softly as he smiled at his soldiers. "I do believe we owe the man an apology, do we not, boys? I say we free him from his shackles and pour him a cup of tea."

The mockery wasn't lost on Gracen, and the look on his face said he didn't appreciate it. I had a feeling that Gracen Lightwood wasn't accustomed to being mocked.

Keep them busy, Gracen, I thought. *And we might just get out of this alive.*

Fortunately, the captain was willing to help as well. "Tell me, Loyalist Gracen Lightwood. Why are you with this colonist?"

"As I previously told you, he is a servant. My steward, specifically. And he accompanied me on a trip. We were on our way home when we were ambushed without warning or cause."

"And where were you before this?"

"Farther South, visiting friends."

I slowly shifted my position closer to the bayonet beside me, keeping my eyes on the soldiers the whole time, stopping when one looked over at me, then resuming movement when they looked away. I kept going until the tip of the bayonet poked into the small of my back, and the ropes around my wrist rested on the sharp blade.

The officer looked at Gracen skeptically, and while all attention was focused away from me, I used the opportunity to cut the ropes. As I sawed up and down, I felt them begin to loosen but knew it would be a while before I could get all the way through. I didn't rush it though. Getting them off was one thing, finding a way out of here something else completely.

And with Gracen tied to a chair, escaping wouldn't be easy. Taking on three unseasoned soldiers was one thing, and we had barely come out of it alive. Four soldiers and an officer were an entirely different issue. Add to that the fact that I had no idea where we were or what would be waiting outside this tent, I knew the odds were stacked against us.

I needed a plan and quick.

"Tell me, young Lightwood," the officer said, his voice even louder than before. "Why haven't you enlisted in the king's army?"

Gracen didn't answer, his silence deafening, his expression impassive.

The officer smiled. "Perhaps you might be more like your colonist friend here than you care to admit."

"Not all men of eligible age have enlisted." Gracen's voice was mild. "I happen to know of several English-born citizens who prefer to show their loyalty to the Crown in other ways."

The captain gave Gracen a look of pure disgust. "Citizens who think they are too good to fight for their king are little better than cowards."

Gracen flushed. "The king knows that my family is loyal, and when my father hears of how I have been treated, there will be hell to pay."

The officer didn't look worried, but he did stand and speak to the other soldiers. "I believe we have given young Mister Lightwood and his *steward* enough to think about. We shall come back later to determine if their tongues have been loosened."

Chapter 10

We were alone for hours, neither one of us speaking, though I wasn't sure if Gracen was staying silent for strategic reasons or because I'd pissed him off. Either way, I used the time to gather information that could be potentially useful.

As the light coming in through the tent changed, then receded, the temperature dropped, making it a little more bearable. The sun had fallen, and although I'd been able to cut through my binds, I stayed where I was, waiting. Thinking.

Based on the voices outside, the soldiers had rotated shifts, the first two having left at sundown. They were replaced by two younger sentries who sounded like boys barely out of high school. I remembered back to when I'd first enlisted and wondered if they were going through the same shock I had gone through the first few nights away from home. Then I realized that they were probably closer to sixteen than eighteen, and a wave of guilt washed over me.

I didn't want to hurt them, knowing well that they weren't responsible for what happened to Gracen and me, but I had a pretty good idea that if I waited any longer, any chance of escape would be gone. I didn't know the details surrounding the aftermath of the battle, and I didn't want to risk us getting caught up in something else. It was now or never, and after listening to the sounds around me, I had a strong feeling that whatever camp we were in, this tent was on the edge of it. If that was true, we could escape through the back and be gone before anyone noticed.

I looked at Gracen, hoping to somehow get his attention without having to speak, but he seemed to be asleep, an incredible feat given the fact that he was still tied to a chair. I just hoped that his limbs hadn't fallen asleep and that he'd be willing to listen to me when I told him to run.

Now that my hands were free, I removed the bayonet from the musket, then whistled to the sentries. They both peeked inside, and I saw that I was right about their age. Neither one looked old enough to shave, which didn't make what I had to do any easier.

"I need a drink," I said, making my voice raspy and weak.

The boys looked at each other, and I could tell they were trying to figure out what to do.

"I'm sure your captain wants us alive so he can question us further, and I've been bleeding a great deal. Some water will go a long way to making sure I don't die in the middle of the night."

The boys – I still couldn't think of them as men – looked at each other. The first shrugged and the second rolled his eyes as he made his way out of the tent to get my drink. I gestured to the other boy, then at my leg.

"Mind taking a look at that?" I asked, letting my head loll over to my shoulder. "The bandage might need to be tightened."

The boy sighed and lowered his musket. I

apparently looked bad enough that he didn't consider me a threat.

I'd been counting on that.

As soon as he was close enough, I grabbed him by the collar of his coat and slid the bayonet into his neck, my hand covering his mouth to stop any sound from escaping. Blood gushed as his body dropped and the bayonet came loose. My stomach churned, but I managed to keep myself from throwing up. I hadn't had a choice. Knocking him out wasn't an option, not when I needed to make sure he wouldn't wake up at the wrong time.

I closed his eyes, looking away as I quickly pushed myself up to my feet. I told myself that he probably wouldn't have made it through the end of the war anyway, but it didn't soothe my guilt.

I limped to the entrance and waited, the bayonet held firmly in my hand. Gracen stirred but didn't wake up, and I silently prayed he stayed that way until I was ready. I didn't need him second guessing what I'd done.

I was doing enough of that myself.

When the second soldier walked in, I waited for the flaps to close and quickly wrapped an arm around his neck, putting the bayonet's tip near his carotid.

"One word," I whispered, realizing I couldn't make myself push the sharp tip through, "and you'll be joining your friend over there."

I turned him slightly so he could see the other soldier. He gagged, and then I slammed the end of the bayonet against the back of his head and lowered the unconscious boy to the ground. I stared at him, knowing I should finish him off, but couldn't.

Giving myself a mental shake, I knew I needed to move quickly, not knowing how long it would be for the next guard shift, and definitely not willing to stick around and find out. I'd been lucky twice today, and I didn't want to push it any more than that.

I heard Wilkins' voice in the back of my mind, urging me to run, to save myself. I hobbled to the back of the tent, and with the tip of the bayonet, sliced downwards, ripping at the fabric while praying I was right about the tent's position. I peeked out through the opening I'd made and was greeted by an empty field with a tree line a dozen yards away.

That's the third one, I thought to myself. There wouldn't be any more lucky breaks for me after this one.

I walked back to where Gracen sat and then took a minute to tighten my bandage. He would have to be strong for the both of us because I was fading fast.

As soon as I started to cut the ropes around his wrists, he snapped awake. For a moment, he struggled, and I was afraid he'd panic and alert soldiers to the fact that something was wrong.

I grabbed his shoulder hard as my hand slammed down on his mouth. He looked at me, frowning in confusion. Then he looked past me at the two soldiers on the ground and all the color drained from his face. I shook him back into focus and then took my hand from his mouth.

"You did that?" he whispered.

"Now's not the time," I said. "We need to go. Can you walk?"

Gracen didn't answer, only stared at the two soldiers lying on the ground, the pool of blood around one of them soaking into the dirt.

"Gracen?"

He finally turned to me. "Yes?"

"Can you walk?" I repeated my question.

He stood up slowly, shaking his legs before

nodding at me. I staggered, and he caught me. For one long moment, I found myself staring deep into his eyes, momentarily mesmerized by them.

It was as if all the air was sucked from the tent as he held me for that moment. Then he blinked and his face morphed into confusion as he looked at me. He shook his head as if trying to clear it and I realized I needed to do the same.

Snap back to reality, sweetheart, I heard Wilkins in my head.

Right. Escape.

Plus, Gracen thought I was a man, so unless he was harboring same-sex tendencies – which based on his confused look, he wasn't – he was simply making sure I didn't fall.

I straightened and pointed at the rip I'd made in the tent. He put a hand on my shoulder and gestured for me to wait, making his way to where I'd been tossed earlier. A moment later, he came back with two muskets and a pouch of lead balls.

"After the last twenty-four hours, I have a feeling we might need these."

"Let's hope we don't have to use them," I said. I didn't add that I was pretty sure I'd have no idea *how* to use one.

He nodded his agreement and led the way out of the tent. We paused outside for a few seconds to make sure no one was scouting the perimeter. When we were confident we could get to the tree line safely, I wrapped an arm around Gracen's neck, and we hurried across to safety. I kept fighting the urge to look back and see if anyone had noticed our escape, fearing that simply acknowledging the possibility would make it a reality. We made slow progress, each step fraying my nerves a little more, but we were soon in the protection of the surrounding woods, and Gracen sat me down against a tree as we stopped to catch our breaths.

"We have to keep moving," I said.

He nodded in agreement, clearly still processing what just happened and I noticed he avoided looking directly at me.

"How far away is your estate?" I asked. It was no longer a question of whether or not I'd go. I had to find somewhere to heal before I could look into getting home.

"Not far, if we take the road past the colonists."

I felt a wave of relief that he wasn't shutting down on me. "I'd rather we didn't cross paths with any more armies tonight."

"Agreed." He smiled at me. It looked forced, but at least it was a smile. "Although to be quite honest, I doubt they'd be a problem for you."

I gestured to my leg. The bleeding had stopped, but the pain was getting worse. "I think I'm pretty much done for a while."

"Then we'll stick to the woods," he said. "Better to be safe."

I nodded, looking back over my shoulder at the camp we'd just escaped. The skies above had started to change color, turning a deep, dark blue. Dawn was a couple of hours away, which probably meant the guards would be found soon. We needed a head start if we wanted to get out of here alive.

"We'd better get going," I said.

Gracen nodded and helped me to my feet, wrapping my arm around his neck again as he grabbed a musket with his free hand. "They know who I am, so they will most likely go straight to the estate rather than trying to track us. Once we're there, my father will contact General Gage and the captain will find himself under inquiry for his treatment of us both."

I thought back to the smile on the officer's face and had a sinking feeling that his scenario might not be entirely accurate. I wasn't going to argue though. "Let's not wait to find out."

Gracen nodded, and we began to move again. The night covered our escape, and as we made our way through the woods, the tension in me started to ease. The danger was far from over, but at least we were heading in the right direction.

Chapter 11

We stuck to the woods, keeping our distance, always alert. The only indication that we were anywhere near danger was the distant voices of colonists in their camps and the lights from the fires. They'd be tending their own wounded, regrouping now, and I hoped they wouldn't pay much attention to a pair of ragged men not wearing uniforms. Well, uniforms that they'd recognize anyway.

As I limped alongside Gracen, the world narrowed down to the next step, then the one after that. I'd hoped for a vacation from my tour and got the complete opposite. Here I was, in the wilderness, looking over my shoulder every step of the way. I was tired, the fatigue setting in quick, my ankle relentlessly assuring me that it was still injured. Between the car accident and everything else that had taken place, I barely had a single inch of my body that wasn't aching.

Gracen stopped us several times, although we both knew that the best thing to do in our current situation was to keep moving. I could see the concern on his face, and I knew his constant need for rests were to make sure I could still make the trek to his estate, even though he didn't say it out loud. I appreciated the generous gesture, especially since I needed it.

It wasn't just the physical wearing on me either. My mind kept replaying the events of the day, particularly the deaths of the soldiers I'd killed. I'd never killed anyone before. Well, that I knew of. I'd fired a gun during a couple skirmishes, but I'd never known whether or not I'd inflicted anything mortal. These deaths...they hadn't been far away, impersonal. I'd taken the lives of those men up close. The first two had been bad enough, but it was the last one, the boy, that I knew would haunt me.

I remembered how Wilkins had always told me that when it finally happened, when I'd be in a situation where the choice was to kill or be killed, I would operate on instinct. That my training would kick in, and it had. I'd felt very little at the time, and I wondered whether that was a good or bad thing. Either way, something in my gut told me that it wouldn't be the last time I'd take a life.

A shudder ran through me, and nausea twisted my stomach.

"You did the right thing," Gracen spoke softly, almost gently. "We both did."

I shook my head, unable to believe him. A part of me began to wonder if there could have been another way, if maybe by morning the officer would have come to his senses and released us without bloodshed.

"We had no other choice."

A hand came down on my shoulder, and I looked up. Gracen's expression was grim, and I wondered if he felt the same guilt over the soldier he'd shot. Was it worse for him since he considered himself one of them? I at least had the comfort of thinking of these men as enemy combatants. Enemies that would've most likely died in this war anyway. Or was it easier? Had Gracen's upbringing prepared him to act when his life was at risk so that he was able to justify it more easily than I did?

But he hadn't killed that boy. Hadn't made the decision to kill rather than incapacitate. That decision had been solely mine, and I wondered now if I'd made it on my own so I didn't have to argue with him. Or if I'd been trying to protect him from what needed to be done.

"How much farther?" I asked, knowing I was deflecting rather than acknowledging what he was saying.

"We're almost there," he said as he pushed himself to his feet. He gave me a ghost of a smile. "I believe you'll be quite pleased with what you'll see."

Even in the dark, the house was impressive.

I didn't know anything about architecture, but I could appreciate the beauty of the structure. Three stories, it boasted at least half a dozen rooms on the second, judging by the number of windows. No smoke came from either of two large chimneys, but the night was still warm enough that they wouldn't be needed. Candlelight seeped through the windows and drapes, the illumination casting an almost romantic glow over the carefully maintained garden and lawn.

Gracen led us to the back, keeping us to the shadows. I didn't understand why, but I didn't question him. This was his place, his time. I had to trust that he would get us to safety. Still, I half-thought he'd march up to the front door and walk in like he was king of the castle, the young Lightwood having finally returned to his not-so-humble abode, announcing his arrival with resolution. Instead, we stopped in front of a nearly-hidden back door on which he rapped softly and waited.

After a minute, the door opened a crack, a lamp illuminating the dark features of a man who had obviously been asleep. The man's eyes widened at the sight of Gracen, and he quickly opened the door all the way to let us inside.

We stepped into a kitchen, and I breathed a sigh of relief. Despite my exhaustion, I was struck by the simplicity of the large space, a stark difference from the stainless steel workplace my mother had recently set up in our family home to replace the homey kitchen I'd grown up with.

When I was a kid, I remembered tearing into the kitchen, clutching my latest artistic endeavor, eager to see it take a place of pride on the refrigerator. I'd tried to hide my sadness when I'd returned from my previous tour to find everything gone, replaced by a collection of twenty-first-century new-age appliances that had looked like they'd jumped right out of a magazine. I'd understood the practicality of the new layout, but it hadn't made me miss the old things any less.

I barely had time to take it all in when Gracen grabbed me by the arm and pushed me along, whispering something inaudible to the man who'd let us in.

We left the kitchen in an inexplicable hurry, climbing stairs to the second floor, then on to the third. He led me to a small room, slowly opened the door, and then gestured for me to follow him inside.

He lit a candle, allowing me to see the small,

simple space. In one corner, right beside a rickety dresser was a bed, the mattress clearly worn but well-kept. He set the candle on the dresser as I sat down on the edge of the bed, my body sighing in relief as I stretched my legs out.

"You can stay here," he said, taking off his coat and laying it down on a chair I hadn't noticed. "It isn't much, but it's safe."

There was a light knock on the door, and Gracen opened it to let the man in. He carried a tray with a bowl and several pieces of cloth on it over to the dresser. He gave Gracen a questioning look.

"That will be all, Titus." Gracen nodded at him.

Titus eyed me for a moment before he nodded and exited the room. I got the impression that the servant didn't trust me, but as long as Gracen did, I was fine. He closed the door softly behind him, sighing as he rested his head against the door.

"What's with the secrecy?" I asked, standing up and inspecting the tray. There was a pungent smell coming from the liquid in the bowl that made me cringe.

"Word will eventually get out about what happened at the camp," he said. "And if my father discovers you here, he'll hand you over without a thought."

"We were both there," I pointed out.

Gracen shook his head. "My father will find a way to make it look like I had nothing to do with the deaths, and that my escape was against my will."

My eyebrows shot up. "He'll say that I kidnapped you?"

"Don't take it personally, Daviot," he said with a sigh. "I will not allow my father to turn you over. You are free to stay here as long as you wish, and when things calm down, I will make sure you get home."

If only he had the ability to make that offer for real, I thought.

He put out his hand. "You saved my life, and for that, I am indebted to you, Mr. Daviot."

I looked up at him, the candlelight casting alternating shadows and light across his features. My eyes traced down across his jaw to his chin, rising to his lips, then up to his eyes again. He frowned at me, and I quickly took his hand. His handshake was firm, from one gentleman to the other, and it took every ounce of willpower within me to stop myself from telling him the truth about who I was. Or at least my gender.

He released my hand. "Until tomorrow, my friend."

I nodded briefly and watched him leave, hating myself for the pang that went through me when the door closed behind him.

I waited for a few more minutes, making sure no one was coming back before I undressed. I didn't even want to think about what that Titus man would think if he saw that I was a woman.

I slipped out of my shirt, wincing in pain as I pulled my arms through the sleeves. The cut on my shoulder had stopped bleeding, but I had a feeling if I didn't disinfect it, it would turn nasty by the morning. I didn't even want to think about what had been on that bayonet.

I got up and made my way to the dresser, taking it easy on my bad leg. As I passed by the small window, I caught a glimpse of my reflection and frowned. My hair was disheveled, my skin streaked with blood and dirt. I unclasped my bra, sighing at the relief of being free of its constraint. I could see the deep red grooves on my skin from where the elastic had dug in.

I dipped one of the cloths on the tray into the bowl, and then tentatively swabbed my wound. Better to get this one taken care of first, then sit down to do my leg. I clenched my eyes closed as pain lanced through my arm. I kept the cloth pressed down though, knowing that whatever was in the liquid was definitely doing more good than harm. After a couple minutes, I dipped the cloth into the bowl again before returning it to my shoulder, the burning less painful this time. I hoped that meant it was working.

I caught sight of my tattoo, the colors of the American flag barely visible in the soft light coming from the candle. I was glad Gracen hadn't seen it. If he had, I would have had a lot of explaining to do.

In the back of my head, I could almost hear my brother's laughter. He'd been with me when I had gotten it, laughing to the point of tears as I'd gritted my teeth to keep from squirming. He'd sat in the chair beside me getting his own tattoo, and although it was a point of pride that his little sister was doing the same, my reaction had amused him. He hadn't, however, teased me about the picture.

We didn't joke about patriotism in my family. Something Bruce had discovered when he'd teased me and taken it too far. Ennis had knocked him to the ground with a single blow.

I stared at the tattoo as I unconsciously cleaned my wound. I knew it would be at least a year before the flag would start to look anything like the one I would come to know. For the first time in my life, the Stars and Stripes wasn't being displayed anywhere but on my own skin.

I finished cleaning my shoulder and then took the bowl over to the bed. I set it on the floor, dunked a cloth into the liquid, and sat down to rest my leg before

I attempted to remove my pants. I knew I was safe here, but at that moment, I would have done anything to be back home. To have my parents with me. I didn't really miss Bruce, which should've said something about the strength of our relationship – or lack of it – but I would've taken any familiar face at the moment.

I took in a deep breath and let it out slowly. I wasn't in Boston anymore, at least not my Boston, and whatever was going on between me and Bruce would have to wait. At the moment, I had more important things to worry about. First, finish tending to my wounds. Then, keep myself from being captured by the British and killed for killing their soldiers. After that, most important of all, I needed to figure out how to get home.

My mind was groggy, though, and fatigue was quickly setting in. I wasn't going to come up with any useful ideas now. I'd be lucky if I got my leg cleaned before I passed out.

There was a light knock on the door, and Gracen let himself in before I could respond.

"Mr. Daviot, I forgot to tell you–"

I sat frozen on the spot as I watched his eyes grow wide. When I registered where his gaze was directed, I quickly grabbed for my shirt as I rushed to cover myself. Heat flooded my face, embarrassment taking precedence over everything else.

Then my eyes met Gracen's and the anger in his gaze made me remember what was at stake here.

Chapter 12

The day I told my family about my engagement to Bruce had been far more uncomfortable than any such announcement should have been.

I'd been ecstatic about the prospect of marrying my high school sweetheart, silently riding a high throughout the day as I had contemplated just how to share the news with the rest of my family. It had been during dinner, when everyone was sitting quietly around the table, offering bits and pieces of conversation about random topics. Ennis had just started talking about the most recent paper he was working on when I blurted it out, like pulling off a band-aid, and the entire table had gone terribly quiet.

I remembered the smile on my face, wide and cheerful, as I'd waited for the rest of my family to congratulate me, to show the same joy as I felt. Finally, my smile had faded as Ennis and my mother had tried to say something, anything, remotely encouraging. Their words had been a mix of mumbles and stutters, my sudden outburst having taken them completely by surprise. They, at least, were trying.

My father was the only one frowning at me, clear disapproval written on his face. He'd never been fond of Bruce, and that night my dad hadn't sugar-coated anything. He'd told me exactly what he thought of my choice, but even if he hadn't said it, I would've known by the expression on his face. I could still remember the way my father had looked at me that night, furious, his hands clenched into fists as he fought hard not to burst out in anger.

Gracen was giving me that same look now.

I sat completely still on the bed, my hands clenching my shirt as I covered myself, just as lost for words as he was. I was barely aware of the pain in my body, only focusing on the man in front of me. His eyes darted from my face to my chest and back again as his lips flattened into a thin line.

"I can explain," I started.

He raised his hand in a gesture that clearly meant that I should stop talking. I could sense his anger from across the room, could almost hear his mind working. I needed to figure out a plan, a story, something to explain the deception.

He whirled around, his back toward me. "Cover yourself," he hissed.

I was about to say that the important bits were covered but thought better of it. Modesty wasn't really the issue at the moment. I pulled my shirt on as I played various scenarios through my head, wondering what this sudden discovery might mean for me now. Whether I liked it or not, I needed Gracen and the shelter of his home, at least for the time being.

I coughed, and Gracen looked over his shoulder at me. Seeing that I was now decent, he turned back around and marched right up to me.

"You lied to me!" His voice was low, but that didn't detract from how pissed off he clearly was.

I sighed. "I didn't lie to you. I just never corrected you."

"You're a woman!" His voice began to rise, his eyes

searching my face as if seeing it for the first time.

I pushed my hair back from my face. "Yes, I am, but if you'd just let me explain."

"What can you possibly say that would make this lie better?" he yelled. He quickly looked over his shoulder at the door, and then lowered his voice. "Do you even understand the consequences of your deception?"

"Consequences?" I asked, frustrated at how much he was blowing this out of proportion. "I saved your life! You said that yourself! How is my being a woman relevant to keeping you alive?"

"You put yourself in unnecessary danger," he hissed. "You could have been killed!"

I stopped my retort, taken back by the concern I could hear mixed with the anger in his voice. Here he was, this man who I barely knew was berating me for putting myself in harm's way, when my own fiancé never even bothered to tell me to be safe. In Bruce's mind, it was pointless to say something like that to someone in a war zone. I had told him that I understood, but I didn't realized until now how much I missed the concern.

"What were you thinking?" he asked as he paced the room. He ran his hand through his hair.

"I can take care of myself, Gracen," I said, deciding not to remind him how I had helped him as well.

"What was I thinking? How did I not see this?" he muttered, and I couldn't quite tell if he was talking to me or to himself. His eyes were fixated on the floor as he paced back and forth, his hand rubbing the nape of his neck. He stopped suddenly and looked at me. "Is Daviot even your name?"

"It is," I said quickly. "It's Honor. Honor Daviot."

"Honor," he rolled my name across his tongue as if

he was testing it. "How ironic."

"Need I remind you that it was *you* who tied me up last night?" I spat. "I was content with going my way on my own. You're the one who kept me by your side like a prisoner!"

"I was protecting you!" he snapped. "I found what I thought was a hurt man lying in an empty field, out in the open, and decided to help. In retrospect, maybe I shouldn't have!"

"Protect me?" I scoffed. "If I remember correctly, we're here right now because of me."

"You're a woman!"

"What the hell does that have to do with anything?" I'd put up with a lot of shit in the army for being a woman, but this was testing my last nerve.

"You lied to me," he repeated. "You knowingly deceived me and led me to believe I was in the company of a gentleman in need of assistance. I risked my own life to defend you. I killed that man to defend you."

"I never asked you to!" I said in retort.

"You never needed to!" he said through clenched teeth. "It was the right thing to do! The honorable thing to do! And now I find out you're a woman."

"So it's only honorable when you thought I was a man? How does that make any sense at all?"

"That is not what I said." He sounded exasperated.

"You're sure as hell implying it," I countered.

"Then you're just as foolish as you are a liar!"

I took in long and deep breaths, knowing that my own spike in temper wasn't helping matters. We both needed to calm down, or things would keep escalating, which wouldn't go anywhere productive.

"I want the truth," Gracen said.

"Excuse me?"

"I want the truth, all of it," he repeated. "I believe

I'm entitled to complete honesty after all this."

I looked up at him, our eyes locking as I tried to weigh my options. How was I supposed to tell him the truth when I didn't even understand it myself? How could I explain to him where I was from, or when I was from for that matter? Considering his clear opinion of women, I had no doubt that he'd instantly dismiss the truth as some sort of hysteria.

But I had to think of something, and he was clearly getting impatient.

"I ran away," I said simply, feigning discomfort, stalling to further develop a fake story in my head.

"From whom?"

"My father," I blurted out, saying the first thing that came to my mind. "I was to be married to a man I didn't love, and when I objected, I was beaten and told that what I wanted didn't matter."

Gracen's expression softened, and I knew I'd chosen the right angle. I watched as his jaw unclenched and the furrows on his forehead relaxed. I felt guilty at having to lie to him again, but the alternative was out of the question. I'd be lucky if I wasn't locked up in a madhouse.

"I couldn't stay," I continued, pushing deeper into my lie. "I had no other option but to run. I knew I wouldn't be able to travel alone as a woman, so I stole clothes from one of my brothers and escaped. I was on my way to Canada, with no food or water, and probably lost consciousness when you found me."

"You were on foot?" Gracen asked, his look showing slight skepticism.

"I couldn't risk taking a horse." I assumed what I hoped was a hurt expression. "My father would be more likely to search for a missing horse than a missing daughter."

Gracen eyed me for a moment, and I could see him trying to decide whether or not to believe me. I prayed he would since I'd reached the end of my endurance. I was tired, my leg ached, and I was worried that if he didn't let this go, I'd pass out before I knew whether or not he planned to turn me over to the British...or just dump me somewhere outside and leave the rest to chance.

I winced as I shifted, and he looked down at my leg, then at the bowl.

"Do you need help?" Color suffused his cheeks.

"I can do it myself. Thank you." I managed not to blush at the thought of having his hands on my thigh.

He nodded, then crossed his arms over his chest. "You shouldn't have lied to me," he said, his voice barely audible.

"I didn't know if I could trust you." That, at least, was honest.

He frowned, an expression of hurt flitting across his face before it vanished. Our eyes locked for a few seconds before he turned away.

"What do we do now?" I asked.

"I cannot condone your actions," he said. "However, I will not meddle in things that do not concern me. Come morning, you can decide for yourself what you wish to do."

I felt panic creep up on me. I couldn't let him kick me out. Not in this condition. I didn't think I'd survive. I needed at least a couple days. "I can cook."

His head snapped up in surprise as he looked at me. "I beg your pardon?"

"I can cook," I said. "I can help out here."

He shook his head. "You have a destination."

"Until my leg gets better, I won't be going far." I pleaded with him with my eyes. "At least let me be useful."

He eyed me for a moment longer before nodding. "As you wish." He turned to leave, his hand resting on the handle of the door as he looked back at me. "I'll send Titus up with proper clothing, and I'll explain the situation to him. He'll keep quiet about our homecoming."

"What about your father?" I asked.

He paused before smiling and saying, "I'll make sure he knows we have a new girl in the kitchen."

With that he exited the room, softly closing the door behind him.

Great. I was a new girl. In the kitchen.

Then again, that was better than British prisoner and accused spy so I couldn't complain. Besides, I wasn't planning on staying any longer than I had to. Once my leg was healed and I figured out how to get home, I was gone.

I didn't belong here, and there was nothing that made me want to stay.

Chapter 13

I spent the next couple days learning every nook of the Lightwood estate as I kept myself busy. I also made sure I stayed in the background. Titus was the only one who knew how I'd come in, and Gracen had made it clear that those circumstances were to be kept quiet. Judging by the look Titus had given me when I first hobbled downstairs in the dress he found, he wasn't too fond of me, but as long as he kept his mouth shut, I didn't care.

After a cursory introduction to the rest of the staff, I'd been put to work. The house was as massive on the inside as it'd appeared on the outside, and every room was richly decorated with antiques and furniture that looked like they belonged in a museum. Except I'd never been to a museum that could hold a candle to this place.

I started in the kitchen, first gathering water from the pump outside before slowly being trusted with more elaborate tasks. It was a tiring business, hours spent just to prepare dinner. My mother had always been a great cook, and I'd always understood the amount of work that had gone into meal preparation. At least, I had in my time. After only one day, I understood why places like this had to have a full staff. One person couldn't have done it all. The servants all worked together like a well-oiled machine. Everyone knew their place and what they were supposed to do.

Which meant it was apparent from moment one that I wasn't a regular member of the staff.

I felt completely out of place no matter how hard I tried. The long gowns I wore were a stark contrast to the uniforms I'd been wearing almost non-stop since I'd enlisted. The way I talked and acted were both out of place and time. I was constantly having to check myself to make sure I wasn't using colloquialisms that hadn't been made up yet. Fortunately, most members of the staff seemed to accept the lie that I'd been born in a more western part of the colonies. Or they were just following the instructions I was sure Titus had given regarding my past.

I tried my best to follow Gracen's advice as well, making sure I said very little, and never about anything personal. There were times I had to ask questions, but whenever possible, I stuck with quick smiles and nods. My leg was healing quickly, but I still hadn't figured out what my plan would be for getting home, so staying here seemed like the best idea for the time being.

That first day, I'd heard rumors that a high-ranking British officer had come by, but since I hadn't been dragged out of the house to face murder charges, I assumed Gracen's father had taken care of it. Still, I kept a low profile.

In some ways, my schedule wasn't much different than it had been in Iraq. Up at dawn, working my ass off, and then, by evening, I would retreat to my room, usually too tired to do anything but lie down on the uncomfortable bed and stare aimlessly at the ceiling until exhaustion caught up with me. I usually spent those last waking minutes thinking about home, about my parents and Ennis, sometimes about Bruce, and more often about Gracen.

I hadn't seen him much since that night, catching quick glimpses of him here and there as I went about my chores. I caught myself staring at him a few times, watching how he moved, the confidence with which he carried himself. When I'd gotten the chance to talk to him, the discussions had been short and quick, Gracen usually asking about how I was being treated before rushing off to attend to one thing or the other. He wasn't cold, exactly, but there was a definite effort to distance himself.

Except I was certain I could feel him watching me. Every time I tried to catch him, he was busy with something else, but I knew he kept looking my way. His eyes haunted me, and at times, I felt as if they could see right through me. Every time he did look my way, I found myself flustered. Half the time, I dropped whatever I was holding or forgot important things. Like my name. Or why I shouldn't just tell him the whole truth about who I was and what had brought me there.

I wouldn't, of course, because I'd already gotten myself into enough trouble. I didn't need to add "crazy person claiming to be from the future" to it.

Sometimes it was like he was two different people. One I'd become vaguely familiar with during our time together outside the estate. The other was the façade I saw for the first time when Gracen had brought in his father to meet the new servant.

Roston Lightwood was the complete opposite of his son. He was shorter than Gracen, but still a tall man. His hair was silver, though I suspected it'd been dark at one time. His eyes were hazel, but the color wasn't the only difference. His expression and gaze were cold, disdainful. He was a man of stature, and he had no problems flaunting it in front of everyone, as if his very life depended on his ability to make everyone around him feel small.

He looked me up and down for the briefest of seconds when he'd first seen me, clicking his tongue as I watched him genuinely size me up, as if I were one of his horses and he was deciding what to do with me. He'd only asked for my name, nothing more, and when I'd given it to him, he quickly dismissed me with a wave of his hand.

Maybe it was wrong of me, but I despised him immediately. I quickly lowered my gaze so that he wouldn't see my emotions all over my face. I didn't know what Gracen had told his father about the "man" who'd killed the British soldiers, but I did know that the only thing Roston knew about me was that I was a charity case who had nowhere else to go. That put me lower than the colonial servants, which was saying something.

He ran the household like clockwork, and the servants were wary of angering him. I'd never seen him angry, but I'd seen his look before, the look of a man who would do anything to get what he wanted and would never take no for an answer.

It was a miracle Gracen had a gentle side at all living under this man's thumb.

"Washington is a madman."

Roston stood firmly in the center of the study,

wine in his hand as he demanded the attention of the room. Gracen sat in a chair beside him, eyeing his father as the older man gestured in the direction of the city.

"As if a ragged bunch of farmers would be a match for the greatest army in the world." Roston drained half of his glass. "Hopefully, this loss will show those rebels that this is a lost cause for them."

I stood to one side in the parlor, my head lowered as Titus whispered instructions to me every few minutes. I moved swiftly through the room, doing as asked, making sure Master Lightwood and his guests were kept content. It took all of my self-control not to show how disgusted I felt, both at what they were saying and at myself for serving them without speaking up.

There were four other men with them, all Loyalists who had gathered to discuss the siege and the battle. I'd already bitten the inside of my cheek a dozen times or more to stop myself from speaking up, the ridiculous accusations and insults being tossed around both frustrating and provoking.

I was pretty sure Titus was hoping I'd slip up and voice my opinions on the matter, maybe get thrown out, or worse, arrested and handed over to the British. What had Gracen called me? A sympathizer? I didn't know if he'd passed that along to Titus, or if Titus had figured it out somehow, but the sideways looks the steward was giving me told me that my placement here hadn't been accidental.

So far, I'd caught Gracen's eye only once throughout it all, and I'd seen the concern there. He didn't need to worry. As pissed off as I was by what they were saying, I had enough self-control to bite my tongue.

Besides, I reminded myself, I knew how the war would eventually end.

"A marvelous victory," one of the guests voiced, raising his glass as if to toast what I knew had been the turning point...for the Americans.

I suppressed a smile as I remembered that the British had lost more than twice the number of soldiers as the Americans. Technically, they'd won, but history would record Bunker Hill as a different kind of victory.

Roston smiled at the man and raised his glass as well. "I almost pity the colonists," he said with a smile. "Then I remember that I have better things to do with my emotions."

The rest of the party – minus one – chuckled at that, and my fists clenched. Gracen looked over at me again, and this time, I knew my true feelings were showing. But it wasn't just anger at what the other men were saying. It was at what *he* wasn't saying. I wanted to yell at him to speak up, to tell them how a *colonist* had saved his life, but I didn't.

It wasn't easy.

"It's George Washington," another man said. "Instilling false hope in these colonists. Some of them are nothing more than peasants, really. A shame, how their loyalty can so easily be manipulated."

"A true gentleman cannot be manipulated," a third chimed in. "These savages had no loyalty to begin with."

"I wouldn't necessarily say that," Gracen said, and for an instant, the entire room fell into an awkward silence. His eyes flickered to me for a second, but no one else seemed to notice, though I suddenly felt like the temperature in the room had gone up a couple degrees. "They are loyal to their cause. I think we can attest to that."

"A lost cause," Roston corrected.

Gracen hesitated as he looked at his father, then nodded slowly. "That may be, but loyalty nonetheless." "Whether these skirmishes end in their favor or ours, we cannot deny that their loyalties lie with their commander-in-chief."

Roston scoffed as one of the other guests chuckled heartily. "Commander-in-chief indeed," the elder Lightwood sneered. "The man's a hooligan and a fake. His followers will notice that soon enough."

"Precisely, Father," Gracen smiled, his voice even. "His *followers*. Certainly, we can call that loyalty."

"I believe, Roston, that your boy has found sympathy for the colonists," one of the guests chuckled. From where I stood, though, I could see the man's eyes, and the look he was giving Gracen was far from amused, despite the fake smile on his face.

Roston noticed it too.

"My son is more loyal to the Crown than his father," Roston said firmly. "If it were not for my sake, he would be standing in the ranks of the king's army shooting rebels as we speak."

"Then why hold him back?" the other man challenged.

Roston took a sip from his wine as he regarded his guest. The challenge had not gone unnoticed, and I could easily see the fury building.

"My son's engagement party is the day after tomorrow," Roston said, his voice strained yet calm. "After that, he is free to do as he pleases."

My chest tightened in a way I didn't like, and I stole a glance at Gracen. His face had gone white, though judging by the similar color of his knuckles, anger, not fear, was the emotion behind it. His lips pressed together, and I knew he was holding back what he really wanted to say.

"In that case," one of the other guests broke through the tension that had risen in the room, "a toast to the young Lightwood."

The other men raised their glasses in unison, and from my corner in the shadows, I tried to tell myself that Gracen's engagement didn't matter to me.

Not. At. All.

Chapter 14

You a different one, ain't ya?"

I looked up from the buckets of water I'd just dragged in to see a young black girl looking down at me. I'd seen her around but hadn't talked to her. And to be honest, my interactions with the rest of the staff had lost what little importance they'd had.

It was the day of Gracen's engagement party, and the preparations for it weren't the only things keeping me awake at night. I hadn't seen Gracen since that night in the parlor, and I hadn't dared ask about him either. Titus clearly felt that what happened had put me in my place, and I wondered if it was less my loyalties and more my relationship with Master Gracen that had concerned him. Though what Titus suspected that relationship was, I didn't know.

I was still trying to wrap my head around the fact that he was engaged, a fact that had kept me up late, kept me distracted when I should've been trying to figure out how to get home. I had no idea why I cared that he was getting married, only that I did. I tried writing it off as some sort of weird bond due to what we'd gone through together, but a part of me couldn't help but feel it was something more.

Not that it could ever be anything other than what it was. For all I knew, Gracen and his wife-to-be were the ancestors of some really important person, and if I messed with that, I'd seriously screw up the world I wanted to get back to.

"Not just your talkin'," the girl said. She eyed me from where she stood, her dress hanging on her lean figure. "Everything about you is different."

I smiled at her, and her eyes widened a bit. I felt bad about that. I'd been trying to keep to myself, so even in the short time I'd been here, I'd developed a reputation for not being the friendliest person. I was pretty sure Titus had done all he could to help me along with that.

"What's your name?" I asked as I straightened. I winced as the movement pulled the still tender skin on my leg.

She wasn't as tall as most of the other women, but I had a feeling it was more due to her age than anything else. She had that lanky look that I had before I hit my last growth spurt.

"Dye," the girl answered.

"I'm Honor," I said, holding out my hand.

She looked at it briefly before taking it, her hold firm as she nodded.

"So, Dye, why do you think I'm different?"

She shrugged, but her eyes never left mine. "You're no colonist," she said. "You ain't from these parts, but you don't sound like no foreigner I ever heard."

I stuck with the story I told Gracen. "I ran away from home, and Master Gracen was good enough to hire me."

Dye shook her head. "You ain't run away from nothin'," she said firmly. "You been brought here."

I frowned, not understanding. "What do you mean?"

"I know runaways," Dye said, "and you ain't one. I

reckon you don't run away easy."

I was about to reply when Titus walked into the kitchen and started barking orders. Dye instantly acted like she'd been busy helping me with the buckets as we trudged to a corner of the kitchen and got to work. I saw her eyeing Titus from where we stood, and when her gaze fell back to me, her expression told me that she wasn't done talking.

I wasn't sure yet if that was a good or bad thing.

The party was beyond extravagant.

Never in my life had I ever seen so many people in such close quarters, flaunting their riches as if competing against one another. The level of sheer narcissism and pretentiousness almost made me gag. The worst part was that I knew people in my own time weren't any different. Even those who protested the war saw nothing wrong with lavish parties and excessive spending habits.

The bulk of guests were gathered in the main dining room, the biggest space in the entire house. I spent most of the morning being taught how to properly set the table. Now, I stood to one side, waiting for a gesture from one guest or the other before rushing to get what was needed, fighting the urge to spit in the wine as I wore my best fake smile and acted as if the condescending tones and barks thrown at me were normal.

Part of me wondered how many of these people

would remain in America after the war ended, if their descendants lied about loyalties the way I knew some people did regarding slavery and civil rights. Had I been fighting to protect the descendants of these arrogant, prejudiced people? Fortunately, I was kept too busy to dwell on those thoughts for too long.

The entire staff was working tonight, the overwhelming number of guests kept us all on our toes, and from the corner of my eye, I caught sight of Dye, the expression on her face telling me that I wasn't the only one needing to practice self-control.

I had to admit though, being in the midst of the upper class during this time period had certainly opened my eyes as to why these people were Loyalists. Everything about the revolution endangered their way of life. While people would always complain about the chasm between the rich and the poor, as well as the problems with immigration, the distinctions of class had gotten blurred in most places.

Despite my desire to announce to the entire room that they were the ones fighting a losing battle, I kept a low profile, making sure I met every snide comment or lecherous glance with a polite smile and nod of my head. My temper simmered just below the surface, threatening to explode with every new insult. At one point during the festivities, I tried to retreat to the kitchen where I wouldn't have to deal with people, but Titus seemed to sense my discomfort and pushed me back out into the melee.

Since I appeared to have no other choice but to smile and bear it, I instead focused on the details. The clothing, the food, the speech patterns. Ennis would've killed for only a few minutes of what I was experiencing. If – *when*, not *if* – I got home, I didn't know if I'd be able to share what happened with anyone, but if I did, Ennis would be it, and he'd want to know everything.

"Ladies and gentlemen, if I may have your attention!"

The chatter quickly died as we all turned toward Roston. He, like almost all of the other men in the room, had donned a wig for the occasion, and it only added to his pretentious manner. I didn't know the proper names for everything he was wearing, but it all looked stiff and heavy, the quality of the material obvious even from where I was standing. For one surreal moment, I felt like I'd fallen into some historical painting or textbook picture.

Then Roston began his speech, and I snapped back to the reality of my present situation.

"There comes a time in every man's life when the happiness of his son is of utmost importance." His voice seemed to echo in the silence, his words reverberating through the room. "That time has come for me, as I stand proudly amongst you all to celebrate my son's engagement to the beautiful Miss Clara Stiles."

A double set of doors to Roston's left opened, and I felt the breath catch in my chest as I saw Gracen for the first time tonight. He was dressed as finely as his father, but the younger Lightwood wore it better. Each cut and line, from his coat to his breeches, told me that the clothes had been specially made for him. He must've been as sweltering as the rest of the people crammed into the room, but his face betrayed nothing. And I could see all of it. He wasn't wearing a wig, but he'd pulled his hair back in the current fashion, somehow managing to tame his wild waves.

He only held my attention for a few seconds, however, as my gaze turned to his fiancée. She was gorgeous, her dress perfectly complimenting her curves even as it dazzled the room. Her sandy-colored hair was piled up on top of her head in a way that made me wonder how long it had taken to get it to stay. Her sapphire eyes moved across the room, clearly taking stock of all in attendance. Her features were fine and delicate, the epitome of feminine.

The minute the couple stepped through the doors, the entire room burst into applause. I forced myself to join in despite the ache I felt. No matter how much I told myself that I should be happy for Gracen, that this had technically already happened, I couldn't stop my chest from tightening, couldn't stop the way my stomach churned.

As I watched the couple stride into the room, my breath began to come in short gasps. The corset I'd been forced into made each inhalation painful and I looked around for an escape. The noise around me became overwhelming, the scent of so many bodies overpowering. I could barely think.

Then, suddenly, I felt a hand on my arm. Dye had already begun to pull me away before I even registered that it was her. I concentrated on staying on my feet, trusting her to take me somewhere safe. As she led my escape, I could hear Roston's voice booming behind me as he started up again. Something about duty and honor that made me want to laugh. I could respect Loyalists who managed to love their home country while still respecting others. I didn't have to know much about him to know that men like him were patriotic because it suited their lifestyle.

I'd seen plenty of his type in my own time.

We came to an abrupt halt as Titus stepped in front of us.

"Where are you going?" He glared at me. "You aren't finished."

"She is for tonight," Dye snapped back.

"Mind your tongue, girl."

To my surprise, she stepped around him, pulling me with her.

"Mind yourself, old man," she said over her shoulder. "This girl is going to be sick from all that noise."

I could barely hear the reply over the second round of applause that echoed from the dining room, and I swallowed hard as I hurriedly followed Dye into the kitchen and out into the cool night air. She didn't ask what happened, or what had triggered my *illness*, but I had no doubt those sharp eyes of hers had caught some of it. Hell, she probably understood it better than I did.

I couldn't be falling for Gracen. Aside from the fact that he was engaged and from a Loyalist family, saying that we were from different worlds was an understatement. In my time, Gracen had been dead for more than two centuries, and it was that time I needed to get back to.

I just didn't know how I could go about doing that.

My feelings for Gracen weren't real. They couldn't be. I barely knew him and I'd never been one who believed in the whole fairy tale thing. I could admit that I was physically attracted to him. He was a good looking man, but that didn't mean anything. I appreciated his good qualities, but that didn't necessarily mean that I felt anything for him aside from admiration and a bit of lust.

I certainly shouldn't feel anything remotely close to jealousy.

Dye took me into my room without asking questions, then gave me a hard look before vanishing back into the hall. The shadows swallowed her up, and I was alone with my thoughts.

Unsurprisingly, I didn't sleep that night.

The last few days had taken their toll on me both mentally and physically, so it wasn't that I wasn't tired. I couldn't feel my feet, and the small of my back ached. My muscles protested the slightest movement, promising me a new round of pain when I had to get up in the morning. I'd always prided myself on being in excellent physical shape, but I was using a whole different set of muscles here.

I tossed and turned, keeping my eyes shut as I tried to force myself to sleep. I attempted to count sheep, to count backwards, to make a list of mundane things that needed to be done, but none of those things were able to overcome the images and thoughts that kept popping up. I couldn't stop my brain from working overdrive.

My mind kept returning to the image of Gracen walking into the dining room with Clara on his arm, the smile on his face like a slap in the face. I remembered the tightness in my chest at seeing them together, the pang of inexplicable jealousy that rushed through me. The guilt and shame that had followed when I'd remembered my own fiancé. Oddly enough, neither of those emotions were focused toward Bruce, but rather toward my own reaction, as if reminding me that I couldn't be upset with Gracen for his engagement since I had a fiancé of my own.

I shook my head in frustration. What the hell was I thinking? How could I feel this way towards a man I hardly knew, a person I had met only a week before? I couldn't wrap my head around it. I knew Wilkins would tell me that it was some love at first sight kind of thing. Destiny or soulmates or some other garbage. I'd given up on all of those things being real long ago. What I had with Bruce might not have been exciting or perfect, but it was real.

I sat up and ran a hand through my hair, shaking it out as I tried to clear my head. The only light in the room was moonlight from a small window, and I walked over to it, threw it open and closed my eyes against the sweet rush of air against my face.

I had to get out of here. It was no longer a matter of making plans or waiting longer for my leg to be completely healed. My survival might not be at stake, but my sanity definitely was.

I sighed heavily as I paced the small quarters, my bare feet cold against the hardwood floor as I hugged myself. I should get dressed and leave right now, no looking back, no second thoughts.

Except I wasn't even having second thoughts. These were first thoughts. Ones that said I didn't really want to leave. That I should stay.

It was ridiculous, of course. This wasn't my time, my life. There was nothing for me here except a job I didn't want, a war that I knew wouldn't end as quickly as Roston and his friends wanted it to. And a man who I couldn't have, no matter what my heart was beginning to say.

I reminded myself that I had a perfectly wonderful life back home. I had a family I loved, a fiancé I may or may not decide to keep and a future in medicine. A future that I'd worked hard to attain. For all I knew, whatever part of the universe that had brought me here in the first place would decide to fix its mistake and take me home tomorrow.

This time, this place, none of it was mine. Whatever happened to Roston, to Dye, to Gracen and Clara, it'd all been finished long before I was born. Their story was already written, and I had no place in it.

Chapter 15

By the time dawn arrived, I was no closer to sleep and felt even worse than before. I couldn't stop thinking about Gracen and Clara, how perfect they'd looked together, how I was sure that if history played out the way it had originally the two of them would be married. And with that came the knowledge that to preserve history, I couldn't interfere, no matter how much I wanted to. Besides, I had my own time – and my own fiancé – I needed to get back to.

It was time to leave.

I knew that I had at least another hour before the household woke up and started their morning rituals, so if I slipped out now, I could be a decent distance away by the time anyone noticed I was gone. I looked about the room, gathering a few things in my pillowcase as I pushed the guilt aside. The Lightwood family was wealthy enough that they wouldn't miss any of this. I needed to move quickly so as not to lose my head start.

Or my nerve.

I opened my bedroom door and peeked out, checking the landing for any sign of servants waking up early. When I was sure I was in the clear, I stepped out, taking care to keep my steps as soft as possible as I made my way downstairs.

As I descended the staircase, my mind tried to reason with me, tried to get me to go back upstairs and forget this whole thing. After all, I had no idea where I was going. This entire endeavor seemed as foolish as it was unplanned.

What was I going to do? Head back to the place where Gracen found me? Even if I could find it, I had no doubt that I'd run the risk of being caught by either army. While I was now dressed as a woman, the officer who'd interrogated me before might remember who I was. They might have old-fashioned notions about women, but that didn't mean they wouldn't hang me for killing their soldiers. If nothing else, it would've solidified the captain's suspicions that I was a spy.

I shook my head as I continued down the stairs. I'd worry about that once I was on the road. The one thing I knew for certain was that I couldn't stay here. It would hurt too much, and I'd be far too tempted to try to change history.

I reached the ground floor and waited, listening for any unusual sounds. When I was satisfied that I was still the only one awake, I made my way down the small hallway to the kitchen. I moved quickly, keeping my eyes on my feet to avoid any missteps. I was pretty sure that women were required to dress like this so that running away would be more difficult.

As I made my way toward the back door, Dye's face suddenly came to mind. I hadn't made any friends here, but if I stayed, she could become one. Part of me wondered if I should have waited another day so I could tell her I was leaving, maybe even offer her a bit of insight into the future so she could protect herself. As noble as that sounded, I knew it was one more excuse to try to convince myself to stay.

I opened the back door and stopped cold when I saw Gracen standing in front of me. His eyes, which had looked half-asleep, widened in surprise, and I swore under my breath. In part, I was cursing my luck, but another part of me was cursing myself. While I, logically, didn't want to see Gracen, my heart went off in a series of skips that made my face flush and my stomach twist.

"Honor." His voice was hoarse. He cleared his throat as his eyes fell to the pillowcase I clutched, and he frowned. "Where are you going?"

I opened my mouth, but nothing came out. I stuttered something incomprehensible as I quickly tried to find an explanation that would both make sense and still hide my true plan.

Unfortunately, he came to the right conclusion before I could manage to speak again. "Are you leaving?"

Scowling, he reached for my sack, and I pulled it back. Technically, the things in it were his, but I needed at least some supplies, even if the only food I now possessed were a couple day-old rolls I'd grabbed on my way through the kitchen.

"It's complicated," I said finally. I could've told him that it was time for me to finish my journey to Canada, but I knew that he'd ask why I was sneaking out. I couldn't give him a reason for that.

Gracen's frown deepened. "Complicated? You're sneaking out while everyone is still asleep."

"I never meant to stay here for long," I reminded him. "It was just supposed to be until my leg healed."

"I know, but I expected at least the common courtesy of a goodbye. You're sneaking out like a common thief." His eyes darted to my bag again. "Is that the truth? Have you decided to rob my family after all we've done for you?"

I struggled to keep my temper. "I'm not a thief. I've worked for my room and board. All I have in here is some clothes and some bread." I held out the pillowcase. "Take it."

He shook his head, color staining his cheeks. "That's not necessary. I'm sorry. I shouldn't have accused you." His eyes met mine, and a thrill ran down my spine. "It's not safe for you out there alone."

His voice was soft, the concern on his face clear. I almost closed my eyes. I didn't want to see that he cared about my well-being because it would be easier to walk away if I could think that I was only a responsibility to him, nothing more. If I knew that he felt anything at all for me as a person, I wasn't sure I could leave.

Even now, I could feel it, the pull toward him, the inexplicable draw that I'd spent the last few days trying to ignore. I didn't understand it, and I was sure that I didn't like it. I knew that I wasn't supposed to like it. Not with Bruce's ring tucked safely away in my luggage somewhere in the future. I always took it off when I was overseas, not wanting to risk it being lost. Now, I wished I'd worn it onto the plane, if for no other reason than as a reminder of who held my heart.

Or, at least, who was supposed to.

I couldn't deny that I wasn't sure anymore.

All the more reason for me to get away before things got even more complicated.

"Please step aside," I whispered. "I'd like to leave."

"No." Gracen practically growled the word. He took a step toward me and my heart thudded wildly against my ribs. "I won't allow it."

"We had an agreement," I repeated. "I'm not a prisoner here, am I?"

"Of course not."

"Then let me go." I had to force the words out of me.

Every fiber of my being screamed at me to stay, to beg Gracen to keep me with him. The intensity of what I was feeling scared me, fueling my need to escape. I'd always prided myself on my independence, on my strength. I never felt like I needed Bruce. I wanted to marry him, and I hadn't liked being away from him, but I'd never felt this inexplicable *need* for him. Not like what I was feeling right now.

The worst part was, I knew it was dangerous, and a part of me didn't care.

Gracen shook his head in response to my request. "Go back to your room and think this through." His eyes narrowed. "Is it because of my father's friends? They're Loyalists, but they're harmless. And no one other than myself knows that your views aren't…similar."

"It has nothing to do with the company you keep," I said. Then I amended it, wanting to be honest with him about this. "Not entirely about them, anyway. This is your house, and I have no say over what happens within these walls."

"I demand a proper explanation." He crowded into my space, his eyes flashing. "I deserve that. After everything we've been through, I deserve an honest explanation."

I looked out the kitchen window at the first signs of daylight and realized that if I didn't leave now, I would have the entire staff to deal with.

"I don't have one," I whispered. I needed to leave. Now.

I tried to push past Gracen, but he grabbed my shoulders, stopping me from going more than a few steps. His fingers burned through my sleeves. I'd never before craved human touch so much.

"Let me go, Gracen," I begged as desperation filled me. Tears burned my eyes, and I struggled not to cry. I couldn't let him know how much this hurt me. "Please, just let me go."

His eyes locked on mine, and those impossible butterflies in my stomach fluttered. The room was suddenly too warm, the air too thick to breathe. His body was less than an inch from mine, and despite the layers of clothing between us, I imagined I could feel the heat of him.

"Gracen," I murmured, unsure what I was asking him to do.

He decided for me as he bent his head and brushed his lips across mine. A shock went through me, and then his hands were sliding up my arms, one to linger on my neck, the other cupping the back of my head. He deepened the kiss, his tongue sliding across my bottom lip. As my lips parted, I leaned into him, feeling his hunger matching my own. I forgot where I was, what I was supposed to be doing. All that mattered was how right this felt.

Then, as suddenly as the kiss began, it was over. He pulled away, and I could see the confusion in his eyes as he stared down at me. This wasn't right, and we both knew it. Even though Gracen didn't know about Bruce, we both knew about Clara, and that alone was enough.

Still, I couldn't lie to myself any longer. No matter how many times I told myself that this was a bad idea, that I couldn't get involved. Hell, it didn't even matter that I'd never believed in the kind of connection I felt toward him. It was real.

And it could never happen.

He lowered his eyes even as his skin flushed a deep red. I wanted to comfort him, tell him it was okay, that it was just a spur of the moment reaction that meant nothing. But I couldn't bring myself to say it, even if it hadn't meant anything to him. I knew, if he decided to kiss me again, I would welcome it and damn the consequences.

"I'm sorry," Gracen muttered, his gaze flicking toward me, and then away again.

I nodded, still unable to find the words I needed to say. There was nothing, actually, that I *could* say. It was all just too complicated.

"I shouldn't have done that," he said, rubbing the nape of his neck. "You're right, Honor, you aren't a prisoner here. But, I beg of you, reconsider what you are doing. It isn't safe out there. You're safer here."

"Gracen," I began but stopped when he held up his hand.

"The choice is yours," he continued, his eyes falling to my lips as our bodies seemed to want to pull together. He looked away. "Just know that if you decide to leave, I won't stop you, and I won't be able to protect you."

With a shake of his head, he brushed past me, leaving me alone in the kitchen with the chaos in my mind.

Chapter 16

I remembered my first kiss with Bruce clearly. I didn't know if it was because it was my first kiss ever, or the fact that I'd been terrified that my father would find out. Or because it was nothing like I'd expected.

Bruce and I had been unofficially dating on and off for a couple years, and while I'd accepted that he'd been too immature to be exclusive, my part of the deal had been that I wouldn't kiss him, or do anything else for that matter, until we were an official couple.

We were in his car, parked in front of my house but away from the living room window where my parents could easily look out and see us parked. A part of me had been worried that one of my parents would draw it open and spot Bruce's car. But they hadn't.

We'd gone to the movies, but I couldn't say what we'd watched. All I could remember was the fact that I'd finally been sitting in the movies with my boyfriend, holding his hand, my head resting on his shoulder as the colors from the big screen flashed across us.

It was one of those teenage things, the perfect first real date with my boyfriend. It didn't matter that we'd actually gone out before, because those outings had been group dates or dances that Bruce hadn't had another date for. This was the first time we'd gone somewhere alone, as boyfriend and girlfriend, and the entire time I'd sat in the theater, I'd known that I would let him kiss me.

We'd gotten home well before my curfew, my father's warning having been given with a smile. The look in his eyes, however, had said it all. He terrified Bruce, and although that had slowly grown old and less amusing over time, it had kept Bruce in check through high school.

It hadn't, however, kept me from getting my first kiss. I'd always imagined my first kiss to be something special, something that would make me shiver every time I thought about it.

Instead, I'd been disappointed.

I'd known, of course, that I wasn't the first girl Bruce had kissed. Kathy O'Neill was all too happy to tell me that she'd received that honor back in seventh grade. In some ways, I'd expected that since he'd gotten in some practice, he'd at least be good at it.

I thought that until his lips touched mine, parted them, and instantly stuck his tongue in my mouth. The kiss was pushy and sloppy, and it took me by complete surprise. What I'd expected to be something soft and sweet, something to show the way we felt about each other, had clearly all been about him. The follow-up hadn't been any better, and when Bruce's hand had reached under the hem of my shirt, he'd been visibly disappointed at my resistance.

Over time, Bruce had gotten better – or I'd gotten used to his technique – and I'd filed my childhood dream of a perfect first kiss alongside things that I'd learned were just fantasies. Like Santa Claus and the Easter Bunny.

I'd also put time travel on that list, and now that

I'd experienced both time travel and an amazing kiss, I was beginning to think that anything was possible.

Maybe Dye had been right after all. Maybe I was here for a reason.

Maybe staying was what I was meant to do all along.

I spent the rest of the day in a bit of a daze, my mind constantly wanting to return to that kiss, to remember the way Gracen's lips had felt against mine. I was next to useless, taking longer than usual to finish my tasks, often earning dirty looks from the other servants, or insults from Titus, but I didn't take any of it to heart. I was too busy thinking about what this all meant. If it meant anything at all.

After lunch, Dye found me in the dining room, cleaning up by myself. I was so busy daydreaming that I didn't notice her until she was standing right next to me, a frown on her face.

"You be a fool," she said, her voice low, but her words sharp.

"Pardon me?"

"You want Master Roston to send you away?" she asked, an eyebrow raised.

It was on the tip of my tongue to say that I actually did want Roston to send me away, but only if it meant I could go home…or that Gracen was going with me.

"You been workin' slower than molasses today."

"I didn't sleep much last night," I said. That was, at least, true.

Dye, however, didn't seem to believe that fatigue was my only reasoning. She watched me work for a few seconds before clicking her tongue and shaking her head.

"You better get what's on yo' mind off it, and soon," Dye said. "Titus ain't happy, and you can be sure he'll tell Master Roston."

I turned toward her, giving her one of my own frowns. "Since when have you become my keeper?"

She clicked her tongue again. "You ain't from here, Honor," she reminded me. "You's a long ways from home, and this place ain't so kind to strangers nowadays. Master Roston wants you out, you gonna be in a spot o' danger."

I stiffened. "I can handle myself."

"Maybe," she nodded, "but when they find out who you really be, they ain't gonna be friendly."

"I'm not a rebel," I murmured.

She gave me a hard look before speaking. "I know. You's so much more. I can see that, and you betcha they will too."

Dye reached down to take the plates I'd collected and walked out of the dining room as I tried to make sense of what she had just said.

By the time evening rolled in, I managed to get myself back on track, picking up my pace while simultaneously trying my best to keep a low profile. It hadn't only been Dye's warning either. I'd bumped into Titus a couple times, and by the second time, I'd gotten a sinking feeling that he was keeping a closer eye on me than usual. Definitely motivation.

I left the study for last, knowing that Roston usually spent most of the day in there, and I was in no mood to interact with the man in any way, let alone hear more Loyalist rhetoric. Besides, if Titus had talked to Roston as Dye had warned me he would, then avoiding him was the better choice.

I opened the study door, then stopped when I saw Roston's back. In front of him sat Gracen, a scowl on his face. His eyes met mine for a split second before they quickly returned to his father. Despite how quick it was, Roston noticed and glared at me for a moment before dismissing me completely.

Apparently, I'd interrupted something important.

"I'm sorry," I said. "I'll come back later."

Roston turned away as if he hadn't heard me, and I backed out of the study, closing the door behind me. I was already starting to walk away when Roston's booming voice came through the thick oak.

"You are being fool hearty!"

I stopped, curiosity getting the best of me. I moved closer to the door but kept my eyes facing forward. I wasn't stupid enough to eavesdrop without keeping an eye out, but I also wasn't about to walk away.

"On the contrary, Father," Gracen's voice was clipped, tight, "I believe I am being quite reasonable."

"You are an Englishman," Roston bellowed. "You cannot have conflicting loyalties. I won't allow it!"

"I do not have *conflicting loyalties*," Gracen countered. "And you do not need to remind me of my heritage."

"It seems that I do," Roston snapped. "I cannot believe we are having this conversation."

"Then why bore yourself?"

"Because you are too stubborn to listen to reason!"

"How is anything you say reasonable?" Gracen raised his voice. "You want me to enlist!"

My heart dropped as a chill ran down my spine. That couldn't happen. Gracen couldn't enlist. Even if he survived the war, he'd go back to England. Thanks to a historical fiction series I'd read a couple years back, I knew how badly the loss had hit England.

"You are a Lightwood!" Roston bellowed, loud enough that I flinched. "We have always been loyal to the Crown and having a son of military age who hasn't enlisted is calling that into question. I will *not* allow our family name to be besmirched!"

For the first time since I had arrived at the Lightwood estate, I felt like Gracen could be in grave danger, and it took all of my self-control not to burst in and tell Roston that his demands would destroy his family.

Roston's friends had often discussed with him what they all believed was a harmless uprising that would be quelled within weeks, or at the most, months. They had no idea what the colonists would achieve, especially in Boston, and that most of them would be fleeing to Nova Scotia to escape the war. The ones who didn't would most likely return to England with nothing. For now, however, everyone was looking for an opportunity to bring honor to their family's name, fight a few battles and return with heroic stories to tell their grandchildren.

Those discussions had obviously gotten to Roston, and now he was willing to risk the life of his only son for glory and honor. I scowled. Bastard.

"I am sorry, Father, but this is one thing I cannot blindly do," Gracen said. "I have agreed to most everything since my birth. This is different, Father. It's a matter of what I believe in, and I do not know how I truly feel about all this."

"What you believe is of no concern to me," Roston shouted, and I winced at the sound of his fist slamming against something hard. The desk, I assumed. "It is a matter of what is right."

"And how is any of this right?" Gracen asked. "How can you stand there and honestly tell me that this battle is right?"

"It is that damn girl that you brought with you, is it not?" Roston's voice suddenly changed, and my heart skipped a beat, wondering just how dangerous it was for me to be standing here. "Since the moment she arrived, you have changed. I never should have let you convince me into hiring that damn colonist!"

"Honor has nothing to do with this," Gracen said.

"She has a name, does she?" Roston sneered. "Don't think I haven't seen how you look at her."

"I am engaged!" Gracen shouted. "Which, I may remind you, is also something I gave into despite my beliefs. And it will be the last time I shall do so."

There was a sudden silence in the study, and I imagined both men staring each other down, neither of them willing to give in. I could only pray that Gracen would continue to stand his ground. The thought of him in a redcoat uniform made me sick.

I needed to find some way to tell him that he was making the right decision, that he needed to stay as far away from the war as humanly possible. I couldn't let him give in to his father's demands. Not about this. I could survive the engagement, but I wasn't sure I could survive it if he died.

Which was ironic, considering a part of me was still trying to figure out how to return to a time when he was already dead.

My mind began to race with all the possible ways I could support his personal rebellion and keep him safe. Somewhere in the middle of it all, a small voice in the back of my head began asking why I'd taken such an interest in his well-being. Deep down, I knew the answer to that, but I still wasn't ready to admit it to myself, as if acknowledging how deeply I felt about Gracen would solidify the wrong I was doing. He was an engaged man. I was an engaged woman. Even if that wasn't the case, there was no future in this, no matter how I felt.

"I need you to make up your mind quickly," Roston Lightwood's voice was unusually soft and composed. "These skirmishes won't last for long."

"I certainly hope not," came Gracen's reply, and with that, I knew the discussion had ended.

I heard footsteps, and then...shit! I was standing too close to the door. As quietly as I could, I raced down the hall and turned towards the staircase, making for the second floor where I was sure I could busy myself with one mundane task or another.

Halfway up, I heard the study door open and close. I couldn't resist peeking over the banister to watch Gracen storm down the hall and out of my sight.

Chapter 17

I dreamed that night.

I was standing in a run-down house of sorts with Gracen by my side. I couldn't make out enough of the interior to tell where we were or even when we were. We were dressed differently, and the air was cold against my skin despite the fact we were inside and I was wearing a coat.

In front of us were a man and a woman standing behind a counter, and I knew instinctively that they were the owners of the establishment. The looks on their faces were disturbing, even a little threatening, especially the scowl that the man had directed at me. Now I didn't know if the chill under my skin was from the look or the cold, but I was extremely uncomfortable.

The woman was talking to Gracen in broken English with what I figured out was a French accent. They were arguing about something I couldn't quite make out, but that was probably because I couldn't take my eyes off the man who was scowling at me. I felt like I should know him from somewhere, but no matter how hard I tried, I wasn't able to place him.

Suddenly, the woman started yelling in French, waving us away. I looked at Gracen, and for the first time, I realized how worn he appeared, a man who had seen and been through more in one lifetime than anyone should. With his hair tied back and tame, he looked very different from the Gracen I knew, barely recognizable.

Still, I knew him, and I knew then that I'd recognize him anywhere. It had little to do with how he looked and everything to do with the way I felt. In that moment, a small burst of inspiration made me wonder if it might have been Gracen who pulled me through time, if this inexplicable connection we had, whatever this was, had been so strong, so powerful, that it broke through space and time itself.

Then the woman's voice rose, joined by the gruff voice of the man next to her, both bellowing in incomprehensible French, and the moment was gone. Despite the tension filling the air, Gracen kept his cool. His eyes briefly shifted to me, as if making sure I was still there, before returning to the couple in front of us.

After another minute, he started talking, and no matter what I did, I couldn't say a word. Now, it was as if I was watching the whole thing through the eyes of a stranger, unable to take part in what was happening. I clenched my fists, fought against my inability to speak, but none of it did any good.

As the shouting faded away, Gracen grabbed my arm, pulling me away as we walked toward the establishment's door. I could see the snow through the windows now, the quick shapes of pedestrians outside as they fought through the cold on their way to their destinations. Wherever and whenever we were, it was winter.

The man shouted something else behind us, and then Gracen's hand was gone. I turned to see him running back toward the man. Before I could understand what he was planning to do, his fist connected with the man's jaw. I tried to scream as Gracen followed the man to the ground, throwing punch after punch, but no sound came out. I tried to run to where they were, but my legs were like lead, my movement forced as if I were trudging through quicksand. All I could do was watch...

I woke with a start, sweat pouring off me, my breath coming in gasps. The room was dark, the night moonless. Instinctively, I reached to the left where my lamp should be, but nothing was there. Mind still muddled with sleep, I reached up to touch the underside of the top bunk. Again, nothing was there.

It came rushing back all at once. The car wreck. Waking up in the past with a stranger watching me.

Gracen.

I closed my eyes again and tried to focus on slowing my breathing. Gradually, my heart resumed its normal rhythm even as quick and sporadic images of my dream flashed through my mind. My entire body shuddered, and as I closed my eyes, I prayed for a dreamless sleep. Just a few hours of uninterrupted, dreamless sleep. That's all I wanted.

"Clara! My dear!" Roston's voice boomed through the house as he greeted his future daughter-in-law. "How wonderful to see you again."

I'd been sent to fetch water, but lingered near the door instead. I'd never considered myself a masochist until now. I knew, despite my daydreaming, that nothing would happen between Gracen and I. I'd given in to my weakness and stayed, but now, knowing that Gracen's beautiful – and appropriate – fiancée was one room over, I had to admit to myself that our kiss was a mistake.

No matter how much it hurt.

"Mr. Lightwood, I thank you so much for inviting me over."

I hadn't heard Clara speak until now, and the sound of it grated on my nerves. I told myself that my dislike was unfounded, that it was the result of jealousy, not of any real reasoning. Still, I couldn't shake the feeling that, should she wish it, Clara could succeed where Roston had failed. And I couldn't let that happen.

Even as Clara and Roston continued their small talk, I forced myself out into the scorching summer heat to do as I'd been told. If I wanted to keep Gracen on the right side of this war, I needed to stay, and to do that, I couldn't shirk my duties.

A small voice in the back of my mind asked when I was going to start worrying about getting home, but I reminded myself that I didn't have any control over what happened. Technically, I didn't even know what *had* happened. It wasn't like the time travel stories I'd read or watched where there was a specific place or person or technology that could be pinpointed as the method of travel, even if it wasn't understood. I'd been in a car accident on a highway outside of Boston. I highly doubted I was the first person to fit that criteria.

I was still thinking about statistics and probabilities when I came back into the kitchen with my water.

"Careful, Honor. Titus, he's got his eyes on you," Dye said as I set the buckets of water in a corner. "You best be keepin' to yourself today."

"He'd best be staying out of my way," I replied, surprising myself with how sharp my words were.

Dye raised an eyebrow and shook her head. I caught a hint of a smile on her face as she leaned closer to me.

"I knows where your loyalty is," she whispered. "It'd be best for you if you found yourself a place with the rebels."

"Believe me, they don't need me," I answered, keeping my voice low.

"I seen you outside the Master's study last night," she continued.

Shit.

She knew I was, at the very least, a sympathizer, and now she knew I'd been eavesdropping. If she put those two together, Roston could have me arrested as a spy.

Hell, there was no *could* about it. If Roston had the slightest idea that I wasn't who I said I was, he'd have me turned over to the British in a heartbeat.

"I was waiting for them to finish so I could clean the study," I explained, slowly turning to look at her. The expression on her face said she didn't believe a word I said.

"You be careful," she said, acting like she had heard nothing of the nonsensical explanation I'd just given her. "Titus be a snake of a man. He think you spyin' on folks, he make your life hell."

I smiled. "I'll keep that in mind."

She gave me a sideways look and shook her head. "You do that. Now, you supposed to ask if Master Gracen and his lady friend want somethin' to drink."

I frowned at the assignment but didn't argue. Dye already suspected that I wasn't who I said I was. If she figured out that I had feelings for Gracen, I knew she wouldn't approve.

I found Gracen and Clara outside on the porch that overlooked the garden. Clara sat on the flowered bench, looking like a porcelain doll in her filmy blue dress, while Gracen stood at the railing, looking out across the carefully manicured paths and blooming flowers.

I paused in the doorway, making myself see the scene objectively, to see Clara as she was and not as I wanted her to be. She was a little older than I knew most unmarried women were, though not quite my age. I was pretty sure that I rated close to being an old maid in the eyes of eighteenth-century society.

She was watching him, and I saw it clearly then, that she wanted him. I couldn't tell if it was love for him, or for his position, but it didn't matter. He'd made her a promise, and when he kissed me, he violated that promise. *I* violated that promise. I didn't know if it was because I hadn't had more than a quick glance at her, or if I was just that awful of a person, but I hadn't truly thought about the hurt that kiss would cause.

I was a horrible person.

I knew how much it'd hurt me in the past when Bruce had been with other women, even though it was before things were official between us. I suspected he hadn't been faithful afterward either. Now, I was that other woman, and even if all Gracen and I had shared was a kiss, it was wrong.

Guilt washed over me, and I turned around to leave the two of them undisturbed.

"He doesn't understand, Clara." Gracen's words stopped me before I'd gone more than a few steps.

"You have to see it from his point of view, my love," Clara replied, her soft voice sugar-sweet. "He sees the larger picture, and wants to guard you against anything that could hurt your future."

"I understand that," Gracen admitted, "but I would feel better if he could see things from my perspective as well."

Perhaps I'd given Clara the benefit of the doubt too quickly. I hadn't heard much of the conversation between Clara and Roston, but now I suspected she was doing the elder Lightwood's bidding.

"You know that he wants what is best for you," she continued.

"You mean he wants what's best for the family name," Gracen countered. "He cares nothing for how I feel or what I want. It's all about reputation."

"You are your name," she said, "your reputation. It's a part of who you are and who we will be. Your father wants you to honor that."

"You sound like him," Gracen said, frustration clear in his voice.

I heard feet shuffling and repositioned myself behind the door so that I could see what was happening. Clara was now standing in front of Gracen, looking up at him as she held his hands. The expression on her face was one of adoration.

"You know I would never side against you," Clara said earnestly. "Whatever you decide, I will support it fully."

"We're to be married," he said, smiling. "How could I choose a war over that?"

Gracen kissed her hands. I wondered if he would feel the same about her words, her wide eyes, if he'd known that she'd spend several minutes talking to his father before meeting with him. Something about this whole conversation made me suspicious.

Clara gave him a smile that made my stomach

turn. Maybe it wasn't only jealousy on my part. Maybe I had a legitimate reason not to like this woman.

"This is hardly a war," she said dismissively. "If you were to choose to join the army, I doubt you would see much battle. Everyone says it will all be over in a matter of weeks, especially after the loss the rebels suffered recently."

If only that were true, I thought to myself. In my time, it was said that inciting the United States to join a war they'd kept out of had been like waking a sleeping giant. History would show that the Battle of Bunker Hill had a similar effect. The loss had fueled the cause, prompting the rebels to continue to fight. We were only a year from the colonies officially declaring themselves separate from England.

"I would have expected you to care more about the wedding than these so-called skirmishes." There was humor in Gracen's voice.

"I care about you," Clara said firmly, "and our way of life. Those rebels are trying to disturb that, and it would do me great honor if my husband were one of the men who put an end to this rebellion."

That little bitch.

Okay, maybe I was being a tad overly harsh. She didn't know what I knew, but I was more certain than ever that Roston had put her up to this. He probably even played the whole prestige card, telling her that if Gracen didn't enlist, once the war was over, he'd be looked down on for his lack of patriotism. If he listened to her, there was a good chance she would get Gracen killed, and all for a way of life that wouldn't last much longer.

At that moment, I hated that I knew the future. Whoever had said that ignorance was bliss knew what they were talking about. Knowing that the British were going to lose this war only made things worse because men died on both sides of the fight. Even if I managed to convince Gracen to switch sides, that wasn't a guarantee that he'd survive the war. My knowledge could only keep him safe if he lived to see the British sent back to England.

No good could ever come out of this.

I turned away from the couple, my mind racing with how to convince Gracen to forget about all this nonsense, to assure him that his neutrality was the best thing for him. If he didn't fight on either side, he wouldn't die in battle, and at the end, his allegiance could be made to America without appearing to be a turncoat.

"You have a way with words, Clara," Gracen said.

I closed my eyes as I heard the concession in his voice.

"I'm not trying to sway you from your beliefs, my love," Clara said. "I just want you to consider your father's proposition."

I opened my eyes and risked another look. My heart sank at the expression on Gracen's face. I didn't need to hear him say it. In that moment, I knew, unless I convinced him otherwise, he'd enlist in the British Army, and some dark foreboding told me that he most likely wouldn't survive.

Chapter 18

Gracen was in the study, alone. He stood at the window, looking out at the setting sun. The skies had already turned a deep red and was now slowly darkening to a shade of purple. The glow coming through the window cast the room in strange shadows, giving the entire room a strange, surreal look.

I wasn't worried about us being interrupted. I'd been cleaning the second-floor windows when I'd seen Roston and Clara walking to the carriage. He'd gotten in, and the carriage had pulled away. I could've assumed that he was merely being polite and seeing her safely home. She planned to marry his son, it only made sense that he'd be concerned for her safety.

Except my gut told me that Roston was more concerned with finding out whether or not she'd managed to talk Gracen into enlisting.

And I couldn't let that happen.

"Don't do it."

Gracen turned around but didn't seem surprised to see me. He didn't look angry or even frustrated. In fact, if I had to describe his expression, it would be one of resignation, and that frightened me.

"Excuse me?" His voice was raspy, and he coughed

to clear his throat.

"Don't join the British Army." I closed the door behind me. While Roston and Clara were gone, the house was still full of servants, including Titus, and the last thing I needed them to overhear was me trying to convince Gracen to go against his father.

Gracen's eyes narrowed. "How did you know about that?"

"None of you are particularly quiet with your discussions," I offered.

He eyed me for a second, frowning, and then his features softened, and he sighed. "You're right. We're not."

I walked over to where he was standing but made sure to keep a respectable distance between the two of us. The last thing we needed was another kiss...no matter how much I wanted it. "Don't do it."

He looked bemused. "Honor, I'm quite surprised by your concern for me, but I assure you, there's little to worry about."

"I doubt that," I muttered.

"I haven't yet decided on my course of action," he said.

"You look like a man who has already made up his mind."

He shook his head as he turned to gaze back out of the window, and relief flooded through me.

"The situation is...complicated, and one I am quite uncomfortable with, despite what everyone says." His voice was quiet, soft. "I truly do not know where I stand, but what I am quite sure of is that this will soon become more than just skirmishes."

I felt relief that he wasn't just buying into all of this, but it wasn't enough. I needed to hear him say that he wasn't going to do it. Part of me wanted to tell him how right he was, how the British might have a couple wins before it was all over, but that, in the end, the British would lose.

I just didn't have a way to explain *how* I knew that without sounding completely insane.

"Maybe you could join me," Gracen teased. "You seem to be quite adept handling yourself, and we both know you can pass as—"

"This isn't a joking matter," I interrupted.

His eyes searched mine for a moment, and I knew he was looking for any sign of amusement. When he found none, he sighed and looked down.

"Very well, Honor Daviot. What would you have me do?"

My mouth opened and then closed again, my mind suddenly blank. I'd been focused on convincing him not to go, wanting him to see that it was in his best interest. Now, however, I didn't think that would be enough for him.

I didn't know why I ever thought otherwise. When I first met him, I thought his not wanting to get involved was because he was hedging his bets or that fighting was beneath him. What I could see now, what I'd seen over the past few days, was that Gracen was actually a man of great principle. He wouldn't support something simply because other people told him he should. He thought things through, considered the weight of his choices.

He wouldn't sit back and do nothing. He just needed to know what he was fighting for. I could see the toll his father and Clara's words were having on him. It was obvious that he was tired of the back and forth, and that he didn't necessarily believe that joining the British Army was important to upholding his family honor.

"Conflicting loyalties, my father calls it," Gracen

continued when I didn't answer him. "It isn't that at all, not the way my father means it. I'm not a coward, Honor."

"I know that," I replied, keeping my voice quiet but firm. "I know you're not."

"Then tell me why I won't take up arms and fight the rebels as my father, my fiancée, and our friends seem to think I should?" he asked, his tone matter-of-fact. "If my father was young enough, he would have enlisted at the first sign of trouble." He paused and then added, "I am supposed to be my father's son."

I shook my head before he even finished the sentence. He was nothing like his father. I knew, in the long run, even if he decided to do nothing, it would save him the heartache of having to leave his home with the majority of the other Loyalists. He could continue here, live out the remainder of his life in peace, an Englishman who had stood on the sidelines, supporting neither side. There was nothing wrong with that.

I supposed, to most people, that was the wisest course of action. It wasn't like everyone in my time enlisted, not even in wartime. I understood that it had to be a personal choice, but for me and my family, there'd only ever been one choice.

We fought.

We might not have always understood our orders, and there were times we might not have agreed with the wars we fought, but we knew that we had to take the bad along with the good. Someone had to stand for freedom and protection, and my family was among those who did it.

How could I tell Gracen that he should remain neutral when I knew that my family, in the same situation, would fight? But how could I ask him to fight for any cause he didn't believe in, regardless of what I knew about the future?

And I knew that I had to admit that my need to keep him away from the fighting had little to do with the knowledge of the war's outcome and more to do with how I felt about him. I couldn't bear to think about Gracen in the battlefield, musket in hand, firing at the enemy as he and the other soldiers stood in perfect lines begging to be killed. I didn't doubt for a moment that he'd only be involved with the traditional form of battle tactics rather than the more covert attacks that some of the American forces would use.

"You'll be killed," I said, my voice faltering as I spoke.

He nodded. "Despite what Clara says, I know that's a possibility." His voice turned bitter. "I can't say that I think my father would be too bothered by it. His only son dying to quench the uprising. Quite an honor."

"That's not funny," I snapped.

"That was hardly my intention." He shrugged. "It's a bit sad, actually."

It was strange, how well I could read him, even after such a short acquaintance. His expression was impassive, but I knew he was thinking, that he was trying to figure out what to do, which course of action would allow him to maintain his principles while not completely alienating his father...or being considered a traitor by everyone he knew and loved.

"Join the colonists."

So...apparently, my brain decided that blurting out those three words to the son of a devout Loyalist was a good idea.

Gracen's head snapped up, his eyes wide. "What?"

No going back now.

"If you feel that you must fight, then join the

colonists," I repeated.

"Are you absolutely mad?" His voice rose as his face flushed.

I quickly looked over my shoulder even though the door was closed. This wasn't a conversation I wanted anyone to overhear.

He understood the gesture and immediately lowered his voice. "Declining to join the British Army is one thing, but fighting with the colonists?" he hissed. "Not only is there the same danger associated with war but to do so will most likely cost my family everything. I could be tried as a traitor, my family name disgraced."

I said the only thing I could think of. "The one thing I can assure you is that your family name will not be disgraced."

"You have no way of knowing that."

"I have a feeling," I lied.

"A feeling!" He barked a bitter laugh as he shook his head. "My father has a *feeling*. Clara has a *feeling*, and now you do too." His voice was harsh as he continued, "Let me tell you a thing or two about *feelings*, Honor Daviot. They are rarely reliable."

He turned away from me before I could answer and rubbed the back of his neck. I hated myself for the look on his face, but I couldn't bring myself to regret choosing to warn him.

"I cannot understand why you would make this suggestion," he said.

"My father always told me that you should fight for what you believe is right," I said. "Can you honestly tell me that you believe the things the Crown has been doing to the colonies is right?"

"It isn't my place to even argue this." His voice rose again.

"Why the hell not?" I asked, my patience wearing

thin. "You know the difference between right and wrong. If you thought the Crown was in the right, you wouldn't even be conflicted about this. You'd have picked up your gun the day the colonists threw tea into the harbor."

He stared at me for a moment before stammering, "H-how dare you even presume to know what I think?"

"I might not have known you for long, Gracen, but I know honorable men," I argued, "and you *are* an honorable man. No one with your family's history of loyalty to the Crown would be standing on the sidelines unable to decide what he truly believed if there was no doubt. You might have conflicting loyalties, but it's not between the British and the colonists. It's between your father and what you think is right."

"Stop it." He shook his head. "Stop talking this instant!"

I couldn't, though, not when I didn't know if I'd get another chance to try to convince him."

"You know I'm right, Gracen," I pressed. "You can't fool me—"

"I said enough!" His voice boomed through the study, and for a moment, he sounded eerily like his father.

"No!" I snapped back. I wouldn't let this go. I couldn't. "Your best chance is with the colonists."

"Why?" he asked. "Why would I join a lost cause?"

"You don't believe that."

"I must!"

"Why?" I asked. "Because your father says so?"

Gracen opened his mouth, hesitated, and closed it again. He glowered down at me, his face livid. I waited, knowing that this time, holding my tongue was the best option. He had to think about what I said, decide for himself if it was indeed his father who was holding him back rather than his own beliefs. After nearly half a minute, he sighed heavily and sank into the chair beside the bookcase.

"I can't do it," he said slowly. "Even if it were the right thing to do, I cannot." He looked up at me, and I could almost see the defeat in his eyes. "I will not disgrace my family. After my wedding, I will enlist in the British Army."

I leaned down and grasped his hand, trying not to let him read the amount of panic flooding through my body. He couldn't do that. I had to find some way to stop him. He looked down at my hands but didn't pull his away.

"You can't do it. It's a terrible mistake."

"Why?" he asked.

"I can't explain it, Gracen," I said, frustrated. "Just trust me that it's a bad idea."

"I need more than something you feel, Honor." His eyes met mine, as if he was searching for something. I just didn't know what.

I gave him the only excuse I could think of. "What about Clara?" I asked. "Do you really want to leave her a widow?"

He raised an eyebrow. "I don't believe that you care very much for Clara."

I refused to dignify that with an answer. Mostly because I had no clue how to answer it.

I tried to stand, but this time, he grabbed my hand.

"Why, Honor? Talk to me."

The urge to tell him everything was overwhelming. I told myself it was because I was tired of pretending, tired of having to constantly be on my guard. It had nothing to do with the fact that I wanted to be honest with Gracen, that I didn't want to lie to him anymore.

I shook my head, fighting back the tears that burned in my eyes. "I'm sorry, I can't."

That searching look again. "You can't, or you won't?"

"Gracen, please, let me go."

"I need an answer." His voice was soft, and it made my stomach twist.

I took a step back, taking my hands with me.

"Why do you want me to join the colonists?" He stood again.

I shook my head. "Gracen, I'm sorry," I said, my voice barely a whisper.

I turned and started for the door.

"Honor!"

I didn't know if it was the desperation in his voice or the fact that it was killing me to hold it in, but I blurted out the essential truth that I needed him to know.

"The British lose the war!"

Oh, shit.

Chapter 19

"I really hate it when you do that."

Wilkins' voice cut through my thoughts and my head snapped up in surprise. Until that moment, I thought I was alone. The bastard had a way of creeping up without making a sound. It was one of the reasons why I was happy he was on my side. That, and the fact that I knew he'd always have my back.

"What are you talking about?" I asked, moving to one side of the broken down wall I was sitting on so that he could sit next to me.

We were in a small town just outside Baghdad, one that had definitely seen better days. The war had taken down most of the buildings, the streets so filled with rubble that barely any space was left for our SUVs to move about freely. If a quick escape was ever needed here, we'd be in trouble.

There were only two dozen people or so in the streets, and we knew most of them. We actually knew most of the people in the town, and many of them were friendly toward us. It was an oasis of sorts for us. A place where we didn't have to be quite on edge.

Wilkins sat down beside me, looking out at where

Rogers was playing a friendly game of soccer with a few of the younger local boys. The big man's burly figure seemed to dwarf them all, but size clearly didn't intimidate them. They hollered and yelled at him as they played, all of them grinning like fools.

"You have this look you get when you're thinking about home," Wilkins said as he pulled out an energy bar and took a bite. He offered it to me, but I quickly shook my head. I was rarely hungry when in the field.

"Is that so?"

He chuckled as he chewed. "I've known you for far too long, Daviot," he said with a full mouth, and I instinctively smacked his shoulder.

It was my way of reminding him to keep his trap shut when eating, but it rarely ever did anything more than encourage him to do it more often.

"Is it Bruce?" Wilkins asked, raising an eyebrow at me.

I shook my head no. "Parents," I said. "I miss them. I haven't called my father in a while, and the last time we spoke, he sounded terrible."

Wilkins took another bite from his energy bar, a thoughtful expression on his face. Rogers waved at us to join him, but Wilkins simply gave him the finger, forcing the big man to laugh out loud. Wilkins rarely moved around unless absolutely necessary, something Rogers and I never failed to tease him about.

"You worry too much," Wilkins said. "It's like you're deliberately carrying the weight of the world on your shoulders when no one's asking you to."

"I can't help it," I replied with a scowl.

"Sure you can. You're not responsible for everything."

"That shouldn't stop me from calling home regularly."

"Your dad's an army man, Daviot," Wilkins said, crumpling up the wrapper and throwing it into the rubble. "He'll understand."

"Do you have to do that?" I asked with a sigh.

"Do what?" He gave a wide-eyed look of innocence that I knew to be a lie.

"Throw your garbage in the street."

Wilkins gestured outwards. "What street?"

"You're unbelievable," I sighed, jumping down and making my way toward Rogers.

"I know you love me, Daviot!" Wilkins called after me.

I replied with a single-fingered salute of my own. I loved him like a brother, but he didn't understand the pressure I was under. Okay, the pressure I put myself under. It didn't really matter where it came from though. It was there, and I had to rise to meet it head-on just like I always did. I took my responsibilities seriously. I always did.

Shit, shit, shit!

My heart was racing, the pounding actually painful against my ribs. My chest tightened, and I was finding it impossible to breathe. I gasped, choked, as I struggled to get air into my burning lungs. I knew I was having a panic attack. I'd had them once or twice before when I'd been on leave. It was like my body stored up all of the stress of being deployed and then released it on me all at once when I was home safe.

That clearly wasn't the case now, because I wasn't home, and I sure as hell wasn't safe, especially after the foolish statement I'd just made.

Whatever else Gracen felt toward me didn't prevent him from trying to come to my rescue. I heard him saying my name, but couldn't answer. He came to me, put his hand on my shoulders. I could see the helplessness in his eyes, and it only increased my guilt.

How could I have been so stupid, blurting it out like that? Had I changed history? Had my careless words altered whatever destiny Gracen had already lived out? What if, instead of saving him, I'd just set him on a course that would result in his death?

When I was a senior in high school, I'd read the short story that had coined the phrase "the butterfly effect." In it, a group traveled back in time, and they're all warned the dangers of straying from the assigned path. One man's failure to do just that results in the death of a butterfly. Something small, insignificant. Except when they returned to their own time, everything had changed.

The concept had been a staple of science fiction even before Bradbury had used a butterfly. If one created a time machine to prevent a death, would saving that person prevent the invention of the very machine that had been used to save them? Can a single moment of bravery in high school completely change the destiny of a family? Will history work to correct itself? Or has our effect already been incorporated into the timeline and we're not actually failing to change history, but rather filling our pre-ordained role?

These thoughts swirled relentlessly through my brain as spots danced in front of my eyes. This wasn't a fictional debate or some theoretical conversation about something that could never happen, because it was happening. To me. To someone I cared about.

"Honor—"

"Stay away from me," I warned as I pulled away from Gracen. My voice was thin, little more than a whisper, but it was there.

What had I done?

"Honor, please, calm down." He held up his hands in a gesture I recognized. He was trying to calm me.

A flash of anger went through me at the thought of him being condescending to me. To my surprise, the anger drove away the panic, and I found myself able to breathe. I gulped in air and closed my eyes, trying to focus on not passing out.

"Talk to me, Honor."

I opened my eyes and saw that he'd come a few steps closer. I shook my head. "You have no idea what I've just done."

He frowned at me, his expression showing his confusion. "You haven't done anything wrong, Honor. You can't be held accountable for your opinions."

I started to say that he was wrong since the British would consider my statement to be tantamount to treason, but then his last word registered.

Opinions.

Part of me was relieved that I hadn't caused as much damage as I'd thought, but another part was angry that he could dismiss what I said so easily. I told myself not to be stupid, that he couldn't know that I wasn't simply stating my mind, but rather historical fact. But that wasn't the real reason I was upset, I forced myself to admit. I might not have been able to expect him to believe me, but I wanted him to take me seriously, to take my opinion seriously.

He reached for me, and I realized that I didn't want him to touch me. Not like this. Not when he was treating me like some fragile, hysterical woman.

"Don't touch me," I snapped as I took a step back.

"It's okay, Honor. You can relax."

"I need to go," I said as I took a quick step around him. "I can't stay here anymore."

"What are you talking about?"

"I've done enough." I was talking more to myself than him now. "I have to get out of here. I should've left the first time around."

He grabbed my arm, turning me to face him. I pulled back, tried to step away, to get away. I needed to go. I needed to get home, to my own time, to the time where this part of history had already been written. I struggled against his grip, and he grabbed my other arm. I was strong, but he was stronger.

"Let go." I stopped fighting and appealed to him directly. "Please, just let me go."

"I won't enlist, okay?" His voice sounded desperate. "I won't go anywhere, okay? I'll stay here."

I was nearly in tears, and I cursed myself for it. He wasn't my responsibility. None of this was. I didn't know the choice Gracen had made originally, and if I changed his mind, for all I knew, I could be changing my entire future. While history hadn't recorded his name, I knew that it wasn't only the people in the textbooks who were responsible for the outcomes of wars. For all I knew, in the history of where I came from, Gracen had enlisted in the British Army, and he'd influenced someone or made some decision that led to a British loss. If he wasn't there, it was possible the Redcoats could win a battle that they'd lost before.

It was too much to think about. Too much responsibility that I didn't want. That I couldn't take. It didn't matter how I felt about him, or that the thought of him dying tore me apart. I couldn't change things.

"I can't...Gracen, I–"

Before I knew what was happening, Gracen's lips were pressed against mine, his hands still gripping me tightly as he drew me toward him. My mind went blank as everything else took a backseat to the feel of his mouth on mine. My pulse picked up again, but it wasn't panic fueling it this time.

For the few seconds we stood there, I felt that time itself had stopped, just for us. That this was the reason

I'd been brought here. I remembered the dream I had, the one where I'd had the epiphany that he was the reason I'd gone through time, that this connection between us had been enough to break the rules so the two of us could be together. For a moment, I believed that none of this mattered, that everything would be okay.

Then he was pulling back, his hands still on my arms. I didn't want to open my eyes, didn't want to see the regret on his face. Because he had to regret it. No matter what my dream had made me think or what my heart wanted, I knew that this wasn't a good idea.

When I opened my eyes, I found him looking at me. Staring with the sort of intensity that made me shiver. I'd seen admiration and lust on Bruce's face. I believed that I'd seen love as well. But I'd never had a man look at me the way Gracen was right now.

"Gracen," I started, but he quickly put a finger on my lips

"Please don't try to leave again, Honor," he whispered. "I don't want you to go."

"It's too complicated," I forced myself to reply. I wanted this so badly, but I knew it couldn't be. "Things are too complicated. Everything is just too complicated."

He shook his head and ran a hand up my arm. His fingers curled around the back of my neck, his thumb stroking across my throat. I knew he could feel my pulse fluttering wildly under his touch. I might be able to lie to him, but I couldn't deny what my body wanted.

My heart wanted it too.

"I don't understand what this is between us," he said softly. "But I can't deny it any longer. I can't lose you. Please, don't leave. It will kill me."

I swallowed hard, my entire body trembling as I tried to fight the emotions coursing through me. I'd tried writing this off as a mere physical reaction. Then as something one-sided. It made it easier to tell myself that it couldn't happen when I believed he didn't return my feelings. I wasn't sure I was strong enough to resist now.

"Tell me you'll stay," he whispered.

"You're engaged." I tried another approach. "No good could ever come from this."

"I don't love Clara," he said. "I never did. This whole engagement was my father's doing. A mutually beneficial relationship between families. Nothing more."

"We barely know each other." I tried another excuse but knew that I was losing the fight.

"Don't ask me to explain what I don't understand. All I know is that I want to be with you. I *need* to be with you."

The hand still on my arm moved to my waist, slid around to the small of my back.

I felt exposed, as if he could read everything I felt for him. Everything I shouldn't feel. My hands came to rest on his chest, and through his clothes, I could feel the pounding in his chest, a quick gallop that beat parallel to mine. I wanted nothing more than to reach up and pull his face down to mine, kiss him until neither one of us could breathe.

Fear of the unknown stopped me. Not only the unknown that came naturally with this sort of thing, but of what consequences might come from my actions. How could I possibly be sure that any relationship with Gracen Lightwood wouldn't change the course of history more than I already had?

"Say something," he murmured.

I took in a deep breath, and then let it out slowly,

looking away from him as I tried to think of what to say. His fingers moved to cup my chin and turned my head back to him. Without hesitation, without concern for consequences, he leaned in for another kiss.

I knew if I told him to stop, he would, but I wasn't strong enough to do it. I gave in, melted against him, and let his touch wash away the doubts and the what-ifs. I stopped worrying and let myself simply be, feel. The hand on my back pulled me tight against him, and I shivered as my body made contact with his. Even through our layers of clothing, I could feel the electricity that flowed between us and knew that this connection between us went deeper than anything I'd imagined possible.

I didn't know who or what had brought me here, or why, but, at least for now, I would stop questioning it. If destiny or the universe or whatever didn't want me with Gracen, then it would just have to send me back to my own time.

Chapter 20

There were moments in life that stuck with a person, some good, some bad. The good ones usually filled me with the same sort of combination of emotions. Excitement. Joy. Often some anticipation thrown in. Each one of them always had the same effect on me though: a longing for the ability to find some mystical pause button that would freeze the moment long enough for me to bask in it for as long as I could.

This was one of those moments. Which, of course, just made it all the more surreal.

As I followed Gracen back through the house and up the stairs, I realized where he was taking me. Okay, so I might've been a little slow on the uptake, but in my defense, I never would've thought a man during this time period would have initiated sex outside of marriage. Then again, it wouldn't have surprised me if I really thought about it. Historically, men often seduced their servants.

I pushed the thought aside. Following it wouldn't go anywhere good. I wanted this. I *needed* this. As he led us into his room, I told myself not to overthink this. And when he turned toward me, the heat in his eyes burned away everything else but the desire for him.

I could already feel my hands shaking as I held back the need to reach out and touch him. My cheeks heated up, and I thanked the dim light of the candles for hiding what would have been an obvious indicator of how badly I wanted him. I could barely understand it myself. I'd always thought I understood attraction, but I now realized that what I'd felt before was nothing compared to what I felt now.

Gracen seemed to glide towards me, a slow movement of his body as his hands reached up to cup my face. Our eyes locked, and it was that moment that I truly wanted time to stop so I could get lost in the waves of color that shifted in the candlelight, lost in the way he looked at me. Capture this moment before real life had a chance to ruin it.

Then again, considering the fact that I was about to sleep with a man who'd been dead for hundreds of years by the time I was born, I'd say my definition of what constituted real life had changed recently.

Then his mouth was on mine, and that was all that mattered.

I hadn't realized I'd expected his kisses to be different now that they were leading to sex until they weren't. There was nothing greedy about them, no desperate attempt to hurry through to get to the main event. His hands didn't even leave my face to try to cop a feel.

My hands curled around his lapels as he broke away from me, and I actually swayed on my feet. Even with my eyes shut, I knew he was close. I could feel his breath against my lips. Every inch of me was tingling.

"What are we doing?" I whispered, my voice cracking. I knew where this would go if we were in my time, but I didn't want to jump to any conclusions. Not with my heart on the line.

One hand slid to the small of my back as the other went around my waist. I opened my eyes to see him staring at me, his eyes almost black.

"What I have wanted to do from the moment I realized that you were a woman," he said softly. "But only if you wish it as well, Honor."

The way he said my name made my entire body shudder, and I set my hands lightly on his chest, the soft fabric of his shirt bending between my fingers as his words pierced through my mind. Only if *I* wanted it too. While Bruce had never forced himself on me, he'd certainly never *asked* if I wanted to have sex with him. It'd always just been assumed unless I specifically said I didn't want to.

"Yes, I want—"

His mouth came down on mine, and I instinctively knew that it came from a need to taste me rather than quiet me. I knew it because I felt the same way. I'd never understood the concept of *need* when it came to another person until now. I honestly felt like I'd explode if I didn't get to touch him.

For the first time in my life, I didn't think about the consequences but allowed myself to dive into the moment headfirst. Gone were the thoughts of Bruce, the worries about Gracen's family and fiancée, the war outside, and the lack of comprehension as to how I was here in the first place. Gone were all my fears, my insecurities, my need to make sense of the world.

All I let myself know was him.

The way his lips moved with mine, the scent of him. The feel of his hair as I ran my fingers through his waves. His broad shoulders, the firm muscles there. My hands slid between us even as his strong fingers kneaded my back. I told him that I wanted this, but I was getting the impression that he was waiting for something from me.

I unbuttoned his shirt even as his teeth grazed my bottom lip. I moaned into his mouth and slid my hands across his chest. His body leaned into mine as I pushed his shirt off his shoulders, his mouth harder against mine, his tongue more demanding. I could feel him hardening against my hip, and then he was taking a step back, his breathing as ragged as my own.

"You're certain about this?" he asked.

I turned around. "I need help with the ties."

His fingers were quick and sure as they moved down my back. As soon as he finished, I turned, not wanting to risk him seeing my tattoo. Just because I refused to worry about all of the other shit going on, didn't mean I'd disregard my safety. The last thing I needed was another slip up.

"Too many damn layers," I muttered as I struggled to get out of the dress and everything else that was under it.

Gracen chuckled, but as the dress finally fell to the floor, the laughter faded, and by the time I looked up at him, his expression was serious again.

"You are a beautiful woman, Honor Daviot."

His gaze ran the whole length of me, one long look that moved over me like a caress. As if my skin wasn't hot enough already.

"So beautiful."

He stepped toward me, the expression on his face not hesitant exactly, but definitely like he was giving me the chance to stop him.

Which wasn't going to happen anytime soon.

His eyes met mine a moment before his hand cupped my breast, and then I was stepping into him. I wrapped my arms around his neck as we fell back onto the bed. My hands moved across his back, gently scratching at him as his lips made their way down my neck, then to my collarbone and lower still. His thumb ran across my nipple, and it hardened under his touch. I arched my back as he kissed his way between my breasts, then moving his tongue across the flesh before taking a nipple into his mouth.

It'd been so long since I'd had any hands on me other than my own, and even then, it'd been so rare that I could already feel the tension coiling inside me. It wouldn't take much for me to get off.

"Gracen," I moaned, and almost as if he could read my mind, his hand moved down between my thighs.

His fingers caressed me, brushed over the dark curls there before slipping one finger between my folds.

"You're wet."

He sounded surprised, and I wondered if the women he'd slept with before hadn't been. If not, it certainly hadn't been due to his lack of skill. His mouth and hands certainly knew what they were doing. I gasped as he slipped a finger inside me, and I opened my legs, allowed him to settle between them.

As he worked a second finger inside me, the world around me dissipated, leaving nothing but the two of us. It was as if we were in a void, an impenetrable bubble where the two of us couldn't be disturbed. He twisted his fingers, and my entire body exploded, rocked by an intense orgasm. I bit down onto his shoulder to muffle my screams, and his body jerked against mine. I heard him mutter an oath and wondered if I'd gone too far. Maybe he wasn't used to a woman enjoying herself.

He pushed himself up on his elbow, his fingers still inside me. He looked puzzled, but not upset. "I didn't hurt you, did I?"

I shook my head. "No, but you're going to kill me."

I groaned in delight as his thumb brushed my clit, my hips now rocking against his hand as his lips traced circles on my neck.

"Is that...pleasurable?" he asked as his thumb touched me again.

I shuddered, hips jerking. "Yes. Oh, fu–yes." I barely managed to catch myself. I wasn't sure if *fuck* was commonly used in this time period, but if it was, I was pretty sure it wasn't something ladies said.

"I'll remember that," he murmured.

It wasn't until I felt the heat of his skin against the insides of my thighs that I realized he'd pushed off his pants at some point. My entire body was pulsing, throbbing, desperate to be filled. I hadn't had anything inside me in too many months to count, and I needed him.

I slid my hand down between us, feeling his stomach muscles jump under my fingers. He drew in a sharp breath when I wrapped my hand around the thick, solid shaft of flesh between us.

"You bewilder me, Honor," he said, his voice low and rough.

I grabbed him by the back of the neck and pulled him closer, my lips locking onto his for one brilliant, hot moment before breaking away. "Is that a good thing?" I asked.

He nodded, lust shining clearly in his eyes. "Very."

I pushed my hips up against him, my hand guiding him to my entrance. As the tip of him pushed against me, I had a second of clarity that told me this was the turning point, the moment that would forever change me. And then his hand was there. He adjusted himself, his eyes never leaving mine, and with one quick push, slid inside me.

A moan escaped my lips before I could stop it, and

I grabbed onto his shoulders tight as he pushed in deeper. My body stretched around him, near painful pleasure that I'd never experienced before. Bruce wasn't small, but Gracen was different, as if his body had been made specifically to fit mine.

He rocked against me, his movements slow, tentative at first, as if feeling his way inside me before moving with more confident strokes. I knew he didn't want to hurt me, and that made me care about him even more. Then the base of him pressed against my clit and the world exploded around me, my mind bursting with ecstasy. I wrapped my legs around him, my nails digging deep into his skin, my hips grinding against his thrusts. He truly was going to kill me, and in the midst of it all, I could feel one orgasm after the other burst through me until I wasn't sure if I was coming multiple times or just one long, unending climax that I was sure would end me.

In the heat of the moment, with my eyes closed and the touch of his lips against mine as we moaned against each other, I could only think of one thing: how much I wanted this to last forever. I could feel the heat of my body against his, his breath against my lips as he moved, his chest pressed against my breasts as our heartbeats raced each other. Emotions rattled my mind, and my moans quickly turned into soft screams that matched his groans of pleasure.

And then Gracen froze, his muscles flexing and his body stiffening. He pushed in deeper with his last thrust, and as he came, I pushed my hips up, reaching for that last little bit of friction. As I felt him fill every inch inside me, I came with him.

After a long moment, he rolled off of me, and his arms went around my shoulders. He pulled me close and brushed his lips against the top of my head. I made sure I pulled the sheet up high enough to cover my tattoo and then allowed myself to relax against him. For the first time since I'd woken up here, all the chaos and tension that'd been keeping me awake was gone, and I let the darkness take me.

As long as I was in Gracen's arms, I was safe.

Chapter 21

"I don't trust him."

My father was frowning, his eyes narrowed. He was angry, and I tried to remember that he was just trying to protect me. It didn't make it any easier to have my father so opposed to my engagement. I wasn't sure why he hadn't seen this coming. Bruce and I had been exclusive for three years, and I'd just finished boot camp. Of course I wanted to be engaged before I reported to Fort Hood.

"You never liked him to start with," I said.

"And I've been clear about why," my father replied. "I know guys like him. I've seen what they do, and who they are. He's not right for you."

I sighed and pinched the bridge of my nose. "How about giving him a chance in the first place?"

"You think I don't know the difference between a man who deserves a chance and a man who doesn't?"

"You don't know him like I do." I gave the same protest that I'd been giving since I'd told my parents that Bruce and I were serious.

"I know his type, and I won't sit around here and watch you throw your life away for him."

"He's my fiancé, and I'm an adult." I didn't feel much like an adult at the moment, but I needed to *remind my father that I wasn't a child anymore.*

"I will not give my little girl to someone who doesn't deserve her!"

It was only then that I saw the tears in my father's eyes. My father who so rarely cried. It was that more than anything else that got through to me.

"You don't get it, Honor." *His voice calmed, quieted.* "There will be moments in your life when you will jump into things based on pure emotion, and when that happens, when the moment is gone and done with, you'll be left with nothing but regret and guilt. I just want to spare you that."

I opened my mouth, wanting to say that I wouldn't regret my decision to marry Bruce, that I knew exactly what I was doing, but the reality was, I couldn't know for sure if I had made the right decision. All I had to go on was an emotional connection to the only boy I ever loved. That had to be enough.

My father was wrong. He'd see it eventually.

I wouldn't let myself think anything else.

"What have we done?"

The moving bed had woken me, but it was Gracen's anxious question that concerned me more. I sat up in bed, wrapping the sheet around my body, the gesture in equal parts to make sure my tattoo was hidden and because I suddenly felt a lot less confident about being naked in front of him. He was half-dressed, pacing about the room like a mad man.

"What are you talking about?" I asked, still dazed with sleep and a little annoyed at the manner by which I had been forced awake. Images of last night flashed through my mind, and Gracen's nervous manner was quickly dampening the sweetness of the memory.

"This!" He gestured to the two of us. "Us. What we did last night. All of this!"

I clenched the sheets tighter to me, instantly self-conscious. I wondered if this was how drunk people felt when they woke up the next day and found a stranger in their bed. I knew we had a lot to work out, but I never expected to wake up to him freaking out. I forgot about how good last night had felt, my thoughts shifting to more urgent matters, like finding my clothes and escaping. I searched the floor, calculating how fast it would take me to get dressed before Gracen freaked out completely. Too long. Damn eighteenth-century dresses.

"A mistake, that's what this was," he muttered, more to himself than to me. "It was a mistake."

Heat flooded my cheeks. "A mistake?" I asked incredulously. If we'd been drunk, I could've seen that explanation, but we were stone-cold sober. We knew what we were doing and who we were doing it with. "I'm sorry, did I trip and fall naked into your bed before you accidentally rolled on top of me?"

Gracen stopped his pacing and glared at me. "This is not a laughing matter, Honor!"

"Do I look like I'm laughing, Gracen?" I snapped back.

"This was wrong. It shouldn't have happened."

I stared at him in utter disbelief, my mind turning with the hundreds of different comebacks I wanted to throw in his face. I couldn't believe how incredibly naïve I'd been, believing that last night had meant something more than just sex.

"You know what?" I finally said. "You're absolutely right."

I threw off the sheet and climbed out of bed, naked, inwardly wincing as Gracen looked away. Bastard. He was obviously ashamed of what we'd done, and while I could understand the ramifications of sleeping with a person while engaged to someone else, he didn't need to be an ass about it. My hands shook as I pulled my dress on, embarrassed that I had lost control of my emotions long enough to get myself into this mess.

"What should we do now?" Gracen glanced over his shoulder and then turned to face me.

I gave him a confused look. "What do you mean?"

"What will we tell my father?" Gracen asked. "How will we explain this?"

I frowned at him. "What the hell are you talking about?" I asked. "We don't have to tell your father anything. It's clear that what happened last night meant absolutely nothing to you, so let's just act like it never happened, and we can both go about our lives."

"Act like nothing happened?" His surprise showed on his face. "How can we act like nothing happened?"

"Just forget it," I snapped back. "This isn't the first time I've seen a man act like a bastard after sex."

Technically, that was true, but I knew it wasn't really comparable. Gracen, however, didn't know that.

He flinched. "What?"

"Did you think this was my first time?" I could hear the bitterness in my laugh. "Oh, don't worry, *Master Lightwood*. You're not responsible for taking my virginity, so don't feel like you owe me anything."

I started to push past him, only to be stopped when he grabbed my arm. My hand curled into a fist, and I barely managed to keep myself from punching him.

"It was a trick," Gracen hissed at me. "Last night was a ruse. You seduced me!"

I yanked my arm from his grip but didn't back away. "You kissed me," I reminded him. "You brought me to your room."

"Trickery," he said, his lips curling in anger. "You

planned it all, didn't you? You intended to get pregnant and trap me into marriage."

I slapped him even as I felt the color drain from my face. I'd never been so humiliated, having someone accuse me of trying to trick...I couldn't even think of it. Tears stung my eyes. It was one thing to hurt over a miscommunication about what last night had meant to each of us. It was something completely different to be accused of something so manipulative and cruel.

The fact that he could think me capable of such a thing told me that I didn't know him as well as I thought I did.

And that my father had been right. Acting on emotion was stupid, and all I had now was regret.

"I have work to do," I said. "Excuse me, *Master Gracen*." I practically ran from the room before he could respond.

I didn't want to be anywhere near him right now. In fact, all I wanted was to go home. My *real* home and time. I didn't want to be here anymore.

Chapter 22

After quickly washing up with the tepid water I had in my room, I changed into my other dress. I didn't linger, didn't look at anyone as I hurried into the kitchen and grabbed the water buckets without being told they needed filled. Titus gave me a startled but approving look as I stepped out into the hot summer morning. He continued to send me surprised glances as I moved from one chore to the other, working with the sort of speedy efficiency I'd learned growing up in a military house. I didn't speak to anyone, didn't make eye contact.

I was pretty sure that Titus assumed it was his influence that had sparked the change, but, the truth was, I only wanted to keep my mind off Gracen. I didn't really care what the steward or anyone else thought of me, not that I knew now what Gracen's assessment of my character was.

I hated myself for sleeping with him, for believing that he'd look at sex with me as anything other than a mistake. I felt like a fool. I'd only known Gracen for a little over a week, and I'd thought we had some sort of special connection.

How could I have been so stupid? How had I let

my emotions get the better of my judgment? I had been careful in the past few years to not let that happen, always trying to make logical decisions, things that could be calculated and planned. I supposed this was what I got for following my heart.

Still, I couldn't stop myself from being a little disappointed when the whole day passed without seeing Gracen at all. I told myself it was better that way, that I needed to cool down, to reevaluate my situation, and to really think about what the hell I was doing here in the first place. And what I should do next.

Gracen had been a distraction, I told myself. I still had no idea how I'd gotten to this time and place, but I'd given the matter too little thought over the past few days. I'd originally told myself that once I knew I was safe, I could take the time to start working through the problem.

Except all I'd really thought about was Gracen and a lot of good that had done me.

By the time evening came around, I'd finished up my work, and the skies outside were turning a bright red mixed with velvet darkness. I'd also finally managed to work the anger out of me.

More or less.

Wiping my hands on a hand cloth, I untied my apron and slumped heavily into the closest chair. It was quiet in the kitchen, and for a moment, I could almost pretend that everything I was trying to forget hadn't really happened.

"Master Lightwood is a happy man today."

Dye's voice came from my right. I opened my eyes and watched her set a couple of empty buckets by the door, ready to be filled tomorrow first thing in the morning. I contemplated getting the task over and done with now before I went to bed, if only to see the surprise on Titus's face.

"He's a smilin' and a toastin' like he be one of dem generals fightin' the war."

I frowned at her, a pang of something sharp going through my chest at the thought that Gracen had spent the day cheerful when I'd been so utterly miserable.

"What's got him so happy?" I asked, wondering if I had possibly missed Clara's arrival. Surely he'd be happy to see his *unspoiled* fiancée. I knew the Lightwoods were entertaining guests; I just hadn't cared enough to find out who.

"The young Master Lightwood, he's gone and joined the Redcoats. Left just after breakfast." She gave me a curious look, as if I should've known.

I felt my heart jump into my throat, and my eyes widen in surprise. Whatever anger I'd felt towards Gracen earlier was now replaced by dread and worry. I looked at Dye in disbelief, unable to wrap my head around what she just said.

"Gracen?"

Dye nodded. "Master Lightwood gots himself a nice bit of attention now," the black woman said in disgust. It was clear where her loyalties were. "Would almost serve him right if those rebels sent his boy back in a box."

I jumped to my feet and grabbed Dye's arm. "Don't say things like that!" My voice came out more harshly than I'd intended.

She pulled her arm away, and I let it go. Her eyes flashed as she stared up at me.

"You's a fool, Honor Daviot. Ain't no place for the likes of you in a Lightwood bed."

My eyes widened even as heat flooded my face. How many people knew what happened between us? He'd acted like what we'd done had been something to be ashamed of, but maybe once I'd told him that I'd had sex before, he'd changed his mind and decided that bedding a servant might be something to brag about.

"You best be findin' your way home, or wherever you going, and leave matters here be," Dye warned, her voice soft. "Dis ain't no place for a girl like you."

I was still trying to figure out how to reply when she whirled around and walked away. I stayed where I was, watching her go. A few minutes later, I retreated to my own room, not wanting to risk running into anyone else.

Unsurprisingly, sleep didn't want to come. I couldn't stop thinking of the many ways Gracen's military venture would end badly, the different scenarios playing out in grotesque details in my mind. He definitely didn't lack bravery, and he had killed that soldier when it came down to it, but I knew that the war would stretch out for years to come. Too much could happen before the end, and even if he survived, his world would be changed forever.

I contemplated running after him, stealing away in the dead of the night and finding my way to where he'd enlisted. I thought that maybe the details would be in the study somewhere, and if I was careful and quiet, I could learn where he was stationed and get him out of there before he got himself killed.

It was my fault, I finally admitted. That's why the guilt was eating me. His enlistment was my fault. We'd been at each other's throats this morning, and now he was gone, off to join the Redcoats in a war they would lose. To spite me, because I'd told him not to do it.

If something happened to him, I'd never forgive myself. I had to find him.

I couldn't just sit here and wait, going about my daily chores as if I didn't know what was coming. I stood up suddenly, making my way to the dresser and pulling out my uniform. I'd found the camouflage pants and shirt the other day, patches of blood still dried from my encounter with the Redcoats. They were clean now. All I needed to do was put them on, and I'd be ready to go.

As I started to pull my nightgown off, my father's words raced back to the forefront of my thoughts. I could almost picture him standing in front of me, frowning in disapproval, warning me of how I was, yet again, letting my emotions get the better of me.

That if I was going to get home, I needed to stop worrying about Gracen and start using my head.

This was absurd. I couldn't do this. I knew nothing of the world outside other than what little I'd read in my brother's books, and even that hadn't been enough for the real thing. In theory, I knew the area, but I knew what it would be like in more than two centuries, not what it was like now.

Shit.

I stared out the small window above my bed into the starry night beyond. I was a stranger here. This wasn't my time, and I knew I'd only made it this far because of Gracen. I wanted to help him, but I didn't know where to start. If Ennis was here, he would've known enough to really help. Me? I read one book years ago. Everything else was what little I remembered from high school. It wasn't much. At least not enough to do what I needed to do.

I balled my fists, feeling my nails cutting into my palms. I hated that I had to acknowledge my helplessness, that I couldn't do this without help. I may have saved Gracen's life, but I couldn't deny that he'd saved mine as well.

Damn you, Gracen Lightwood.

I was angry at him all over again. I was angry at how he'd made me fall for him, how he'd taken my attention away from the more important matter of finding my way home. How he'd just up and left me behind without so much as a goodbye.

And I hated myself more for caring about any of it.

I sank back onto my bed, the anger draining as quickly as it came. I couldn't take any more of this. I might not know what I wanted to do about re-enlisting or about my idiot of a fiancé, but at least there, I had family, a place I knew.

I had to get home.

That was the only solution. I had to find some way back home. There was nothing for me here, not that there should be. Whatever delusions I momentarily had, whatever false opinions I'd used to shroud the truth, I couldn't do it anymore. This wasn't my home, and it never would be. I shouldn't be here.

I had to find my way back.

Chapter 23

"Why's you lookin' at me like dat?"

Dye stood completely still in the kitchen doorway, buckets in her hands, eyeing me suspiciously as I watched her. I shook my head slowly and then went back to what I was doing.

I wasn't entirely sure what I expected, but when I finally managed to fall asleep, my dreams had been full of flashes and chaotic images. The only thing I could remember when I woke, however, was that I needed to talk to Dye. She was my ticket out of here and back to where I belonged.

Now that Dye was actually there, I couldn't think of how to even start explaining what I needed from her. Hell, I didn't entirely know what I needed. She'd always been a little curious about me, and I wasn't completely certain that she hadn't somehow figured out my secret. If she knew, then it was safe to assume she might also know how my time jump had occurred and might even know what I could do to reverse it, because if she understood traveling through time...

It made my head hurt.

Yet now, in the kitchen with all the other women, with Dye casting suspicious looks in my direction, I found it hard to approach her. What could I even say?

I had no idea where to start, especially if I was wrong and Dye knew nothing.

Maybe the girl was just extremely intuitive, and in reality had no idea what I had been through. It was clear I was out of place, that I didn't belong here, but it didn't take a genius to know that. Maybe Dye just had a knack for saying the right things at the right time. In some ways, she reminded me of the gypsy ladies during carnival season back home.

"If you gonna keep lookin' at me dat way, I best be makin' maself pretty," Dye said, as she dried her hands. "You got somethin' to tell me, Honor?"

I looked over her shoulder at the other women around us, noticing how some had edged their way closer to us and were eavesdropping on our conversation. I wondered how many were listening for anything they could pass along to Roston, and how many were looking for gossip about me and Gracen.

I made a decision. "Not here," I said. "Outside at the well." If she didn't know anything, then I'd be back at square one, but at least I'd know I was doing whatever possible to get home.

Dye smiled at me and pushed a bucket in my direction. "Good," she said. "We got us a few more of dese to fill."

I watched until we were standing at the well, buckets by our side, before I asked the only question that mattered. "What do you know about time travel?"

"Whatcha mean by *time travel*?" Dye pulled a blade of grass and chewed on the end of it as she leaned against the well.

"Moving through time." I chose my words carefully. "Like going to the future...or the past."

"Now why'd anyone wanna do dat?" she asked, regarding me shrewdly. "Past's better left alone, and future's comin' whether we likes it or not."

"That's not what I meant." I straightened and stretched the muscles in my back. Being active in the army meant I was in shape, but it didn't mean I wasn't feeling it. I struggled to find the words. "What if someone traveled in time without wanting to? Like they were forced into it, and they couldn't do anything about it."

She eyed me for a beat before she clicked her tongue and laughed, a rich, full sound. "You speakin' nonsense, Honor," she said. "The sun's getting' to ya."

"I'm serious." I refused to let it go. "What if someone wanted to go home? How would they do that?"

She spat and scratched her scalp, looking off at the extensive grounds of the estate as if looking for the answers around us. In that moment, she looked less like a young servant, and more like some sort of wise woman. The hairs on the back of my neck stood up, and I was certain that she would have answers for me.

"You's been chased from home, dat it?"

All the air rushed from my lungs, and my shoulders slumped in defeat. For some reason, I'd thought this would all be over soon. That Dye would have answers for me, and I'd just follow them. I'd be home in no time.

"Dat your explanation for actin' strange all day?"

"I wasn't chased from anywhere, Dye," I said, exasperated. I ran my hands through my hair. "I actually like my home, and I want to go back."

Dye's head snapped toward me, and she eyed me for what seemed like forever, as if trying to decide whether or not I'd completely lost my mind. Finally, she shook her head.

"You ain't never made any sense, Honor," she said. "I know dis all about Master Gracen runnin' off to dem

Redcoats?"

"This has nothing to do with Gracen," I quickly argued.

"I ain't a fool," Dye said. "I seen da two of you together. How he always be lookin' at you, even when he pretend he don't be. It's a miracle Master Lightwood and little Miss Clara ain't got a clue, or you be in some serious trouble."

"Nothing is going on," I said again.

She raised an eyebrow. "You's sure about dat?"

"Positive."

"Den must've been someone else I heard hollerin' in his room dat night." She grinned at me.

I froze, my eyes wide as her words sank in, and I could immediately feel the heat rush to my cheeks. Shit. How the hell could I talk my way out of this one? Dye chuckled when she saw the look on my face and waved her hand at me.

"If I could count 'ow many times white men sleep wid da help, I be countin' 'til kingdom come."

I grabbed the pump handle and started working it again so I wouldn't have to respond. My night with Gracen couldn't have been like that. He wasn't like that. The fact that he'd freaked out so badly was an indication that he wasn't in the habit of sleeping with random women. But if anyone else knew about our night together, they'd assume I was just one in a long line of servants who warmed his bed.

I frowned. I didn't really care what anyone thought of me, but I hated the idea of anyone thinking poorly of Gracen. Then again, maybe sleeping with the staff would be something that Roston would consider manly. He seemed like he'd be that sort of chauvinistic asshole.

"So you be feelin' guilty and wanna run away," Dye continued as if her statement explained my question.

I shook my head, even though, deep down, I knew that Dye's words were probably truer than I wanted to admit. I didn't want to think about that though. I couldn't think about Gracen right now. I needed to focus on getting home.

"Is there magic that can send me home?" I asked, hating myself for the desperation in my voice.

"A horse can take you home, girl." She smiled at me. "Ain't need no magic for dat."

I stopped what I was doing and looked up at her. "Dye, I'm serious."

"I's as serious as you, Honor," she countered. "You ain't need to go meddlin' in things you know nothin' 'bout. Ain't no magic gonna erase da past, and ain't no magic gonna bring da future. You best be leavin' it at dat."

I sighed, trying to hold back my frustration, knowing I was getting nowhere with this conversation. I needed to try something else. Suddenly, I remembered the volumes of books lining the shelves in the study. Maybe I could find answers there. I just needed to find a way to get my hand on them without being noticed. I was pretty sure Master Lightwood wouldn't think too kindly of any of the help touching things that didn't belong to them.

I stifled the sudden and completely inappropriate laughter that wanted to come out. I'd definitely touched something that didn't belong to me.

"Finish up wid dem buckets," Dye said, breaking through my thoughts. "I gonna take dese two in wid me."

I nodded at her and continued pumping. With a new goal in mind, I could at least feel like I hadn't given up.

The next few days went by uneventfully as I settled back into a routine. Dye and I chatted, but I didn't bring up time travel again. There was clearly no point. I was, however, still looking into other possibilities. Fortunately for me, sneaking books out of the study and to my room proved to be a simple task. The reality was, no one even noticed anything was missing. I simply left cleaning the study to the very end of the day, polished it off and then escaped before Roston Lightwood and the rest of his Loyalist friends filed in. It was easy hiding a volume or two in my dress, and none of the men gave me a second look.

They were all too busy congratulating each other on the imminent downfall of the rebel colonists.

It was exhausting. I spent days working and stealing books, hours of the night occupied with reading. Well, technically skimming. I wasn't a slow reader, but it was a lot of reading. There was very little in regards to time traveling or the mystical, but the work helped keep my mind off Gracen as well as the ever-growing frustration of not being able to find a way back home.

It didn't keep me from thinking about Gracen, wondering how he was faring with the other soldiers. I didn't know anything about how the army worked in this time, especially not the British Army. Gracen had been gone less than a week. I didn't know if he would have had time to train, if he'd be put somewhere out of the way and safe, or if he'd be sent straight to an active unit, one that would be in the very middle of the danger.

I'd tried eavesdropping, but there was very little information on Gracen. The only mention of his name was accompanied by the pride Roston felt at his son's patriotism and loyalty. I was surprised at how well I controlled myself considering the anger I felt whenever I heard Roston bragging.

This wasn't my fight. Even the war itself wasn't my fight. It'd already been won. My priority was getting home to my family...and to my fiancé, of course.

Bruce.

Groan.

I was a little embarrassed to admit that I'd hardly thought about Bruce since I'd arrived here, and I had to keep reminding myself about him even as I looked for a way home. The man I was supposed to marry occupied very little of my thoughts despite the trouble I'd gone through with my family to fight for him. It was strange that it'd taken something as drastic as this to make me reevaluate my choices.

As June drew to an end, I still hadn't made any progress, and it was wearing on my nerves. The fact that I'd also heard nothing about Gracen only made matters worse. By the time the sun set on the last night in June, I was barely holding it together. I had no idea what I was doing, was no closer to answers, and was starting to think that the smartest thing I could do would be to head west, get as far away from the coming battles as I could. I knew enough about roughing it to survive, maybe even do well, in this time.

As I plopped down on my bed and stared up at the ceiling, I wondered if it was time to just accept that unless whatever had brought me here decided to send me home, I was stuck.

Either way, I couldn't stay here any longer. I needed to do something other than wait on the

Lightwoods. So, when I was sure the entire household was asleep, I quickly gathered my things and shoved them into the pillowcase. It took less than a few minutes for me to change back into my uniform and head downstairs. This time, I knew I wouldn't turn back.

Gracen wasn't here to stop me.

I walked swiftly, leaving the Lightwood estate behind me. I'd give it one final try before I accepted that I was here to stay, and I knew that meant I had to go back to where it all began. As I made my way back toward Boston, I wasn't sure what to hope for. A way home, or a clear sign to stay.

Chapter 24

I stayed close to the road, just within the tree line, yet far enough to avoid detection unless someone was looking very closely. The night was cooler than I remembered July nights to be, but that could've been because I was comparing it to Iraq – or because Boston was warmer in my time. The moon was almost full, allowing me enough light to make my way forward, which I appreciated since the territory wasn't familiar enough for me to move both quickly and stealthily. I measured my steps carefully, trying to make as little noise as possible while keeping my senses sharp for anything out of the ordinary.

I was grateful for the concentration, however. It kept me from worrying so much about Gracen. It was sad, and more than a little annoying, that my brain was more focused on where Gracen was and how he was doing than it was on getting home. I told myself it was because time travel was a bit more mind-boggling than guy problems. My subconscious was trying to deny the impossibility of what happened to me.

Yeah, and I believed that bullshit as much as I believed in the tooth fairy.

Then again, I'd never believed in time travel until I'd found myself in 1775. Maybe I'd meet Santa Claus on my little trek.

On and on I went, one foot in front of the other. Not once did I consider returning to the Lightwood estate. After all, there wasn't anything for me there. Not anymore.

I had no idea how long I'd been walking before I finally stopped to rest, slumping down next to a large tree. My legs ached, and my feet hurt. I felt like I'd been going non-stop since I'd gotten here. One thing after the other, with barely any time to even breathe.

I took the time to breathe now, but I didn't find any peace from it. After so many months in the desert, the air smelled strange to me, the almost wet scent of trees and grass, but I knew that wasn't the only reason. The lack of the signs of humanity that I'd always associated with back home weren't here. Car exhaust. Lights. Pavement. Even overseas, I'd never been completely away from any of it.

Suddenly, I realized that I was hearing something other than the usual nighttime rustlings of forest animals.

Hooves. Coming this way, and fast.

I jumped up from my resting spot and hurried a few yards deeper into the woods. There, I crouched down and waited to see if it was friend or foe. If I could even tell such a thing. Now, I registered the sounds of wheels as the carriage came around the corner, and I hoped it meant I wasn't about to see British soldiers rounding the bend. A carriage most likely meant a civilian. At least, according to the minuscule bit of knowledge I'd gleaned from movies and TV shows over the years.

I ran through my options, wondering if this might be an easier way for me to get to my destination. Maybe a safer way. I had no idea who was inside the carriage, and there was no telling whether or not they would stop, much less allow me to join them. Still, it had to be better than walking the entire distance, and I was a little wary of what might happen if I got too close to an army camp. I might know the dates and outcomes of a few battles, but I didn't know troop placements or daily strategic operations.

Before the carriage could pass me by, I decided to go with the lesser of two evils. I jumped up from my hiding place and sprinted through the trees, angling my path so that I stepped out into the moonlight with enough space to spare as it jolted to a stop.

The man sitting up top driving the horses let out a stream of curses that tempted me to flip him off. Instead, I held up both hands to show that I didn't have a weapon. I didn't want to risk trying to guess which side the owners of the carriage were on, so I went with saying nothing.

After a moment, the carriage door opened, and the pungent aroma of whiskey and cigars drifted out to welcome me. The moonlight didn't offer me a clear look at the inhabitants, but it was enough for me to get an idea of who was inside. I saw a portly man sitting opposite a beautifully dressed young woman.

"What is the meaning of this?" he bellowed, clearly pissed.

To my surprise, the young woman – maybe even young enough to be considered a girl – slapped at him with her fan, frowning angrily as he turned toward her. She slapped his knee with her fan again, and I watched in amusement as the man huffed and looked away. She turned to me and smiled widely.

"Excuse my father," the girl chirped. "He is in quite the mood today."

"No apologies necessary," I said back, trying to keep my voice as deep and masculine as possible.

"May I ask what a young man such as yourself is doing out here in the middle of the night?" she asked, her eyes dancing.

Right. Young man. Especially in the dark, there was no way someone would mistake me for a woman.

"I'm on my way to Boston," I said. "I was wondering if perhaps I could trouble you for a ride if you were going that way."

"Do you take us for fools?" the man snapped at me. "You will rob us and leave us here."

I heard the sound of a gun clicking and turned to see the muzzle of some sort of pistol pointing at me. I was pretty sure that he'd only have one shot, and it'd take a while to reload, but I didn't want to consider what would happen if he ended up being accurate with that single shot.

"Come now, Father." She kept her eyes on me. "He doesn't look like a criminal."

"They never do," her father muttered, eyeing me scornfully. "What is your business in Boston, boy?"

"My business is my own," I said politely. "But I would be much obliged for your assistance."

The man's eyes narrowed. "What side do you take in these...disputes? I don't wish to make enemies–"

"Oh, Father, you see rebels and redcoats behind every rock and tree nowadays." The young woman turned back to me and gave me an even more brilliant smile than before. "Of course, we can assist you."

Her father glowered at me as I climbed into the carriage, but I didn't get shot or hit, so I was satisfied for the time being.

That lasted until about two minutes into our trip when it became apparent that the young woman – Elizabeth, she insisted I call her – was more interested in whether or not I was married than actually helping out a stranger. It took everything I had to maintain a smile while simultaneously keeping as much distance between us as possible...which was difficult since she kept finding excuses to shift in her seat so her dress would brush against my leg.

It was one thing to have a lesbian flirt with me and have to politely say that I wasn't interested. I had no clue how to handle the attention from someone who thought I was a man.

While the journey was short and uneventful, Elizabeth's attentions and her father's glowers kept it from being pleasant.

She chatted non-stop about parties and dresses, and how much her family's popularity had risen despite recent events. If it had only been prattling about this and that, I could've simply smiled and nodded, feigning interest while barely paying attention. But that wasn't enough. She wanted to know about me too. Her questions never stopped coming, and I worked hard to be as vague as possible, even after I discovered that they were Loyalists. I didn't want to risk leading them back to the Lightwoods.

I had to admit, as I listened to her talk, that it was a bit surprising how few people believed these 'rebel skirmishes' would amount to anything. To Elizabeth and her father, this was all just a game that would quickly come to an end once the British really put their minds to it.

Ennis told me once that people used to say that the sun never set on the British empire because the Brits had colonized so much of the world that, at any given point in time, the sun was shining on a place that Britain claimed as its own. After listening to Roston Lightwood and his friends, and now Elizabeth and her father, I could understand how such a saying had become popular.

I wondered what they would say if I told them, come August, King George would declare the colonies in official rebellion, and things would quickly escalate from there. Probably the same thing Gracen had done, I knew. They'd think it was a dangerous opinion to have.

And then they'd probably throw me out of the carriage.

It was actually a little sad, once I allowed myself to truly think about it. Sure, there were arrogant people who treated the colonists like second-class citizens and wanted England to defeat the rebels so they could remain in power and comfort. But there were also those who deeply loved their country, who didn't want to be a part of a new one, but rather an equal member of the country they'd always thought of as home.

War was never simple, I reminded myself. Something that wouldn't be any different in my time.

I thought of the internment camps in America during World War II. The innocents who'd died in the bombings of Hiroshima and Nagasaki. The Germans who'd faced persecution and death even if they hadn't supported Hitler's regime. The Vietnam War and the horrors that had been committed by both sides.

Then I thought about the war I'd fought in. One that had started the moment a few hate-filled individuals had murdered thousands of Americans. Nearly nine years later, we had no end in sight, and people were questioning the wisdom and morality of what we were doing.

No, war was never simple.

Even with all of these thoughts bouncing around in my head, I kept my mouth shut about politics. I probably would've made a better impression if I'd agreed with them, but I couldn't bring myself to do it. It would've felt too much like a betrayal. The best I could do was keep silent.

As soon as we passed through the siege line, I interrupted Elizabeth's description of her latest dress.

"If you'll excuse me." I gave a polite smile to both Elizabeth and her father. "I believe I'll walk from here."

His eyes narrowed. "Are you a rebel soldier, boy?"

"No," I said as I leaned closer to the door. If he tried to stop me, I'd make a jump for it. Hopefully, they'd be too worried about the Colonial Army to try to go after me.

"Then we'll take you into the city." Elizabeth said it like it was a done deal. "You certainly don't want to be left out here with those rebels." She sniffed, her pretty face twisting into something unattractive.

I shook my head. "I appreciate the ride, but I'd like to stretch my legs a bit. They're stiff from sitting so long."

I didn't add that I knew things would be fairly calm for the rest of the year. There'd be some minor skirmishes, some raids, that sort of thing, but the city would stay as it was until the new year. After that, the British would withdraw and the Americans would have the city. The major danger had passed, so I'd most likely be safe between the Colonial Army and the city limits.

Besides, this was where Gracen had found me, so even if it wasn't exactly safe, if I ever wanted to get home, this was where I had to be.

The carriage had slowed to a walk as the road began to curve. I remembered this area and knew that I had to get out now or I'd never find my way back in the dark.

"If the ungrateful bastard doesn't want to ride with us anymore, I say good riddance."

Before I could respond, Elizabeth's father pushed open the carriage door and unceremoniously shoved me out. I heard Elizabeth give a scream of protest, but I was more concerned with curling my body so that I landed on my shoulder rather than my face.

By the time I got up, my shoulder and arm throbbing, the carriage was several yards away. At least I'd managed to hang on to my pillowcase of belongings, I thought as I stretched myself out, checking to make sure that some bruises and scrapes were all I had. The cut on my shoulder felt tender, but I didn't feel any blood, which was good. I couldn't, however, say the same for my leg. The wound there had been deeper, so it was taking longer to heal. Even in the dim light, I saw a few new dark spots on my pants, but it could bear my weight.

I sighed. I needed to find somewhere to sleep for the rest of the night. I wasn't sure of the exact spot where Gracen had found me, so I'd need to walk every inch of the area and hope that I tripped something, and it took me back to my time. If I didn't find anything by the time my food supplies ran out, I'd change into the one dress I'd brought and go into the city to decide what to do next.

With a set plan in my mind, I looked around for the best possible place to steal a few hours of sleep. My journey, I knew, was far from over.

Chapter 25

I woke with a start at the touch of a hand on my shoulder, and immediately kicked out, registering a cry of pain when I connected with something. Muscle memory took over even before I'd fully woken, and I twisted away from the hand, pushing myself into a crouch, hands curled into fists. My breaths came in gasps, my heart beating like a hammer in my chest as adrenaline coursed through me.

"Honor, stop!"

I froze at the familiar voice, staring as Gracen held up his hands in surrender. It took my brain a few seconds to catch up and allow my body to relax. Still, I couldn't quite believe he was here. My mind whirled at the odds, the incredible improbability of this man finding me in this same place two separate times. Fate had to be at work.

And he looked like shit. His clothes were rumpled and dirty as if he'd been sleeping in them for a while. His hair was wild, and there were even bits of leaves in his hair. His skin was pale, except for the dark circles under his eyes.

What the hell had happened to him in the week since I'd last seen him?

"Gracen?" I finally managed to say his name.

He smiled at me, but it was a weak smile and didn't quite reach his eyes. "Honor, what are you doing here?" He sounded even more tired than he looked, which was saying something.

"I could ask you the same question," I countered, my mind still reeling. I believed I'd never see him again. "Why aren't you with your unit...I mean, your regiment?"

He looked away, a dark flush creeping up his neck. The realization hit me all at once.

He'd never joined the army. That might have been what he told his father, but he'd never actually enlisted.

"Did they recognize you from before?" I looked around, wondering how much danger we were in.

He shook his head, giving me a quick glance. "I didn't give them the opportunity to. How could I after the things you said? How passionately you believed them?" He looked at me now. "I am an educated man, Honor, and I've never been one to believe in the superstitions of others...but something about how ardently you argued for your cause..." His voice trailed off for a moment, and then he finished his thought. "It almost made me believe."

I had absolutely no idea how to respond. Despite my best efforts, I hadn't been able to completely keep myself from thinking about what I'd say if I saw him again. It'd seemed like such a remote possibility that I told myself no harm could come of it. Except it had, and now that it was here, my mind was inexplicably blank.

"You have no idea how happy I am that you're here." His voice broke through my thoughts. "I never thought I would see you again."

"Then why did you leave in the first place?" I

asked. Maybe it was an inane question, and I had a feeling I'd hate the answer, but I asked it anyway. I needed to know for certain.

The conflict was written on his face, and a part of me was glad that I wasn't the only one going through such emotional turmoil. It would've been worse, I thought, if it'd been easy for him to walk away. If I hadn't meant enough to him for it to be painful.

"Gracen?" I prodded. I didn't know if I'd get another chance to ask him, so I was going to push until I got an answer, no matter if I liked it or not.

"I couldn't stay there anymore." He looked at me, his eyes blazing. "Not while you were there."

I rolled my eyes. Was he serious? First, he said he was glad to see me, then he said he couldn't be near me. Men. I gave an exasperated sigh. "Do you know how contradicting you sound right now?"

"I know, I know," he said as he ruffled his hair and turned away. "This hasn't been easy for me."

"Easy for *you*?" I stared at him, unable to believe what he just said. Anger sparked inside me, burning past everything else to set free the words I'd held back. "Do you have any idea what I've been through since you decided to disappear?" I let every negative emotion bleed into my words, but managed to keep my tears back. "I gave myself to you, trusted you, and when you didn't like what you heard about me, you accused me of being a manipulative slut!"

His eyes were wide when he turned around. "I never said–"

"You might as well have," I snapped. I wanted all of this out. I needed to have it gone. So I could have closure before I went home. "As soon as you heard you weren't the one who took my precious virginity, you immediately jumped to the conclusion that I'd seduced you to try and trap you in a marriage."

He at least had the decency to look embarrassed. He started to reach for me, then dropped his hands. "I apologize, truly I do. I wasn't myself that morning. The whole thing took me quite by surprise, and I admit that I didn't handle it well."

"That's an understatement," I muttered. I folded my arms, determined to keep strong. "You acted like a...child, and then ran away."

"I couldn't think of a better solution."

I resisted the urge to roll my eyes but didn't hold back what I was thinking. "That wasn't a solution, Gracen, that was a fear of confrontation." I let the silence sit between us as I rubbed my arms. I hadn't realized until now how early it was, how the sun hadn't yet burned off the chill. When I finally spoke, my voice was soft, "Do you have any idea how much I hated you for leaving like that?"

His shoulders sagged, and he leaned against a nearby tree, a defeated look on his face. I didn't understand him, didn't understand what he was thinking. He'd stood up to his father about the war, but had fled when faced with having to explain what happened between the two of us.

Maybe I didn't mean enough for him to show that sort of bravery and strength. The thought tore at me.

"What were you expecting would happen?" I asked, taking a step closer. "That you could pretend to your father that you were in the army and when all this was over go home like nothing had changed?"

I wanted to tell him that he'd have years to wait if he thought that.

"I didn't have a plan," he admitted, his tone wry. "It seems that I do unwise things when I'm around you."

I winced as his comment and rubbed my forehead.

"And what were you thinking – or not thinking – that I'd be doing during all this? Or did you even care about that at all?"

Gracen looked up at me. "I care. How could you even question that?"

I stared at him. Was he serious? A thought occurred to me. "Did you think that when all this was over, I'd be waiting for you at the estate? Waiting for you to come back?"

He waited for a moment before answering. "I prayed you would be."

He wasn't kidding. I could see it on his face.

"How could you possibly think that? Any of that?"

Gracen sighed and closed his eyes.

"Do you have any idea how bad–?"

"I was married once."

The statement stopped me cold. I looked at him, but his eyes were still closed.

"Her name was Silva," he continued. "She was seventeen when we married, but I'd loved her since she was thirteen."

I sat on the ground across from him, watching. Waiting. I wasn't sure I wanted to hear him talk about this woman he'd loved so much. I knew it couldn't have a happy ending, not if he was supposed to marry Clara now.

"We had only been married for a few months when she told me we were expecting our first child. We were so happy. Even my father was happy, and I'd never seen him happy before." His eyes opened, but the look in them said he was far away. "I supposed he must've been, with my mother, but I was too young when she died to remember him that way."

"What happened?" I didn't want to ask it, but I had to know.

He finally looked at me. His words were quiet,

even. "She died in childbirth, and our son died with her. In one night, I lost everything. Everyone I ever loved was gone." His voice broke.

Without thinking about it, I crossed the short distance between us and wrapped my arms around him. He stiffened at first, then relaxed against me. I held him close, cradling his head against my chest and buried my face in his hair as tears welled up in my own eyes. I wondered if he'd ever let himself cry for his wife and child, or if his father had made that impossible too.

"I never thought I would be able to love anyone like that again." Gracen's voice was muffled until he pulled back and met my gaze. "Until I met you, Honor Daviot."

I swallowed hard. I couldn't let myself hope that he meant what I so desperately wanted to believe he meant.

"Forgive me, Honor." He cupped my cheek, his eyes dark and shining. "Forgive me for all of those horrible things I said to you."

Tears escaped and ran down my cheeks. I couldn't do it. I couldn't pretend that this wasn't happening, not anymore. I'd been fooling myself into thinking that what I had with Bruce was real. *This* was real. More real and pure than anything I'd ever felt in my life.

He leaned into me, resting his forehead against mine. I closed my eyes and concentrated on the feel of his thumb against my cheek, the heat of his breath on my lips.

"I love you, Honor Daviot. With every thread of being inside me, I love you."

I gave in to what I wanted, what I needed, and closed the distance between us to put my mouth against his.

Chapter 26

He loved me. There was no pretense to it, no prompting or reason why he should say it. He didn't have anything to gain by saying it. Which was why I believed him.

And why I knew I had to leave.

I broke the kiss and took hold of his hands. I squeezed them as I took a deep breath. I had to do this before I lost myself in him. It would be so easy to do, and it would only hurt him in the long run.

"I...I can't..." My throat started to close, not wanting to utter the words. I made the mistake of looking into his eyes. Confusion and hurt stared back at me, and I didn't know what to say next. I pushed myself to my feet and took a step back.

Gracen stood, a bewildered expression on his face. I knew he didn't understand what I was doing or why I was doing it. Hell, I barely understood it. I only knew that it was right.

"You can't what? I don't understand."

I turned away from him so he couldn't see the tears in my eyes. I picked up my pillowcase but didn't bother getting out any of the food I'd packed into it. I wasn't hungry. I wasn't anything. I wasn't even thinking in terms of going home anymore. I just wanted to be done.

"Honor, stop!" He grabbed my arms tight enough to hurt. "Please, just tell me what–"

"I love you too, Gracen!" The words burst out of me, as if I simply couldn't hold them in any longer.

A smile broke across his face, and it was the most beautiful thing I had ever seen. This was what real love felt like, and it was tearing me apart. I knew what I'd felt for Bruce had never been true love because the thought of never seeing him again didn't cause me any pain.

But what I'd say to Gracen next was going to rip out my heart.

"I'm going home, Gracen." It physically hurt to say the words.

"But you love me," he countered. "We can be together."

"And do what?" I asked, forcing myself to be strong. "Go back to the Lightwood house where you can marry Clara and I'll spend the rest of my life watching you have a family with her? I can't do that. And I won't be your mistress. I'm going home."

He released my arms, and I nearly fell.

"You said your father beat you. Why would you go back to that?"

Shit. I'd forgotten about that.

I pinched the bridge of my nose. I could come up with an excuse. I was sure I could. But I wasn't sure I wanted to anymore. I was tired of lying.

An inkling of an idea poked into my mind. Maybe I could do it all at once. Tell the truth...and push Gracen away enough that leaving him would be easier.

"My father didn't beat me," I said finally. "He's one of the greatest men I know. I lied to you before because I couldn't tell you the truth."

Gracen took a step back as my words sunk in. His eyes narrowed, and for a brief moment, I saw a glimpse of his father in him.

"You've never stopped lying to me, have you?" His hands curled into fists so tight that his knuckles turned white. "Has anything you've ever said been true?"

"I couldn't tell you the truth – I still can't – you wouldn't believe me." I knew I needed to stop trying to explain myself. I needed to accept his anger and leave. But I didn't like the idea of his last thoughts of me being that I was a liar.

"You owe me the truth." His voice was calmer, but I could see the anger in his eyes. "If you love me, try."

Fuck. I couldn't get any air into my lungs, even though I could hear the heavy panting of my labored breathing. Black spots appeared in my vision, and I realized that I couldn't do it. I couldn't just feed him a lie and walk away. If he was going to hate me, then it had to be because he truly knew who I was and where I was from.

"Sit down," I murmured.

"I'll stand."

I nodded. My legs couldn't hold me anymore, not now that I'd made the decision to come clean, so I sat. I rested my elbows on my knees and stared at the grass.

"No matter how crazy this sounds, please let me finish, because I don't think I can get through it more than once."

When he didn't argue, I took that as the closest to an agreement I was going to get.

"These clothes I'm wearing are the uniform of the United States of America." I could feel his eyes on me. There was no going back now. "I joined the army in the year 2004, shortly after I graduated from high school..."

I explained everything, and he let me talk. I told him about Iraq, my unit and Wilkins, everything I had seen and done overseas, everything that had set me on the path that had eventually led me to him. I told him about Bruce, and how long we'd been together, hoping he'd figure out that my fiancé was the only other person I'd slept with. I couldn't bring myself to specifically say it, but I wanted him to know anyway.

And then I told him what I knew of this war. Of what happened to the British Empire and how America grew into a powerful nation. I kept my voice even, forced myself to detach from any of the emotions that wanted to come forward with the memories.

When I finished, I felt drained, empty, but a little better. At least, no matter what happened, I'd know that Gracen knew the truth. I glanced over at him, but he was staring at the ground. I wasn't sure when he'd sat down, but he was less than a foot away now. Physically, at least. I knew he was a hell of a lot further away in every other sense.

The sun was almost directly overhead now, but I didn't ask him to hurry. It was a lot to take in. I'd lived it, and I barely believed it.

"If you didn't want to tell me the truth, you could have at the very least been respectful." His voice was soft but angry.

"You can't think I made all this up?" My chest tightened. It wasn't unexpected, but it still hurt.

"I don't see any other explanation for it." He stood and started to walk away. "I'll leave you be since that seems to be what you wish."

"I can prove it!" I called after him as I scrambled to my feet. That little voice in the back of my head that had been telling me to walk away was getting smaller.

As he turned, I grabbed my shirt and yanked it

over my head.

"What are you doing? Cover yourself!" Gracen snapped as he turned. His face flushed, but I couldn't help noticing that his gaze kept snapping down to my bra-clad breasts. It was a simple white cotton bra, but by eighteenth-century America standards, it was extremely revealing.

That alone should have been a hint to him that I wasn't from around here, but it wasn't what I wanted to show him.

I took a breath and turned around. I bent my head forward so that my hair wasn't in the way. It took a moment, but then I heard him gasp. I gave him some time to adjust to the side of a tattoo on a woman, and then another minute while he absorbed it.

"What is that?"

I glanced over my shoulder to see him coming toward me, his eyes locked onto my shoulder. "What does it look like?"

He looked up at my face briefly, and I nodded for him to continue, giving him permission to touch me. A shock ran through me as his fingers touched my skin, tracing the lines of the American flag he didn't recognize.

"It looks like a flag," he said quietly. "But not one I know."

"This is what the flag of the United States of America will look like in the future. In the time I come from." I closed my eyes and tried to focus on the truth of the matter rather than the way his touch made me feel.

"Tell me."

I swallowed hard and prayed that this meant he was starting to believe me. "The stars symbolize the fifty states that will make up the USA. The stripes are the thirteen colonies that will all eventually declare independence from Britain. Soon."

I looked at him again. His face was pale, eyes wide.

"I swear to you, Gracen, everything I told you is the truth. Including how this war is going to end."

I watched the emotions play out on his face. Confusion. Anger. Grief. I waited, determined to give him the time he needed.

He stepped closer and traced the lines of my tattoo with his fingers again. Then he bent his head and pressed his lips against the nape of my neck. It sent a shiver down my spine, and I had to remind myself not to get caught up in the physical.

"I believe you."

The relief that went through me at those three words nearly made my knees buckle.

"Can you forgive me?"

I turned toward him, and then his arms were around me, and I felt safer than I had in a long time.

"Will you?" he murmured against my hair. "Honor, my love, will you forgive me?"

I nodded, not trusting myself to speak. He believed me. A lot of things still needed to be figured out, but for right now, in this moment, this was all that mattered.

How long we clung to each other, I didn't know, but when I finally raised my head, it was to see Gracen's face flushed, his eyes looking everywhere but down at me. He took a step back, retrieved my shirt, and held it out to me. I pulled it on, then glanced over to see him staring out into the distance, a confused expression on his face.

"What's wrong?" Anxiety twisted my stomach into a knot. I really hoped he wasn't going to tell me that this all had been a mistake. I wasn't sure I could handle it if he did.

"What's a car?" he asked.

A laugh burst out of me, and I was surprised to realize how long it had been since I'd genuinely laughed. After everything I had told him and everything I had confessed, he asked about the car. I shook my head. Typical man. My father and brother would've approved.

He looked a little annoyed as he turned to look at me. "I need to know what a car is if I am to try to understand how you came to be here."

"A car is like a much faster carriage," I explained. I gave him a soft smile. "I'm sorry I laughed. This whole thing is just crazy.

"Are cars inherently magical?" The question was asked as calmly and seriously as someone would've asked about the weather.

"No." I studied the grave expression on his face, wondering where he was going with this. "Why?"

"You had no expectation of being transported anywhere but to your home." He made it a statement rather than a question.

"Correct."

He scowled. "When I found you, you were hurt, disoriented and had just been in a carriage accident that unexpectedly placed you in a different time. And my response was to tie you up and treat you as an enemy." He shook his head. "I cannot blame you for trying to get away from me."

I walked over to him and placed my hands on his cheeks, turning his face toward mine. "We were both in an impossible situation that neither of us could be expected to know how to handle."

Of all the ways for him to react to the truth, I'd never thought he'd blame himself for any of it. I remembered Wilkins telling me once that I carried the weight of the world on my shoulders. I was beginning to see that I had nothing on Gracen.

Chapter 27

I leaned in to kiss him, to reassure him that I didn't blame him. He needed to know that none of this was anyone's fault. Before my lips could touch his, he took a step back, turning his face from mine.

The sickening realization hit me as I dropped my hands. My biggest fear was coming true right in front of me. Telling him who I really was had changed how he felt about me. It'd just taken him a couple minutes to realize it.

My stomach lurched, and I could feel the pain already starting to bubble up. I moved farther away so he could have the space he so clearly wanted. It would kill me to leave, but at least now I knew for certain that I had nothing to stay for. I wouldn't marry Bruce – I couldn't now that I knew what real love felt like – but I would at least have my family.

"Sorry," I whispered. "I understand if, after everything you've just heard, you don't want me anymore." My voice faltered on the last word. I couldn't believe I'd been so stupid. Whether he believed me or not, it was a lot for anyone to handle. Too much apparently. After being honest about everything, I'd lost him anyway.

As I started to turn away, Gracen moved. Except

he didn't move away from me. Instead, he closed the distance between us with two long strides and grabbed the tops of my arms, forcing me to face him. His hands rose to my face, and he used his thumbs to brush away the tears that had begun to fall.

"Look at me, Honor." His voice was earnest, and I raised my eyes. "It does not matter where or what time you are from. I want you, and I love you. Nothing will change that. I swear it on everything I hold dear."

He kissed me then, pouring more love and passion into it than I'd felt from Bruce in all the years I'd known him. I slid my arms around Gracen's neck, ran my fingers through his hair. His touch was gentle, but I felt the strength in him, the restraint he used not to be rough with me. I leaned closer to him, wanting him to lose control, but he pulled away instead and brushed back a loose strand of hair.

He kissed my forehead, and I took the opportunity to get the air my lungs demanded. I'd experienced fear in various forms in my life, but nothing as intense as what I felt when I finally told Gracen everything. The risk had been worth it, even though I knew there was one more thing I had to say about it.

"Can you forgive me for lying to you?" I asked. He'd asked for my forgiveness, but I needed his as well.

"There is nothing to forgive," he whispered, resting his forehead against mine. We stood like that for a moment and then he straightened. His expression was tight when he looked down at me. "Do you still want to go back?" he asked. "Back to your own time?"

I opened my mouth, then closed it when I realized I didn't have an answer ready. What did I want?

I felt a twinge of sadness as I thought about my father and the guidance that he gave me, whether I wanted it or not. I considered my loving mother who'd supported me going into the army when she knew the risks. My older brother who'd been equal parts friend and nemesis. I was used to not seeing them for extended periods of time, but the thought of never seeing them again was different.

And it wasn't only my own feelings I had to take into consideration. I didn't know if I could leave them without answers. Without a goodbye. They were probably worried sick. If time was moving the same here as there, I'd been gone for almost a month. I didn't know what answers they had, but I knew they wouldn't be enough.

The honest answer was that I didn't know whether I wanted to go home or not, but I did know that I didn't want to lose Gracen. Could I choose him over my parents and brother? Over my military friends Wilkins and Rogers?

"If you wish it," he said quietly, "I will do everything in my power to see you safely home."

I could hear the effort it took to speak those words, see the pain in his eyes, and I knew in that moment that he loved me more than Bruce ever had. What I wanted, what I needed, was more important to Gracen than anything else.

"We will explore all possible sources of information," he continued, clearly taking my hesitation as an answer. The only hint at the inner turmoil he was feeling was how tightly his hands were clenched. "Some of the servants may have mystical knowledge."

"I spoke to Dye before I left," I said almost absently, "and she said she didn't know anything."

I couldn't waver. Not now. This was the moment where my life would take one path or another. I couldn't say how I knew it, only that I did know, deep in my bones. I could no longer leave it all on chance. I had to decide whether or not to actively pursue finding a way to get back to my time. And I knew that no matter what I chose, I would lose people I loved.

I knew what I truly wanted, even if I hadn't wanted to accept it until now.

"I love my family, and I miss them–" I started.

"Then we will search for a way home for you," he cut me off. He was all business now, unable to look at me, unwilling to show his pain.

"Let me finish," I said gently. He nodded, the muscles in his jaw clenching. "I love my family, and I miss them...but I can live without them." He inhaled sharply but didn't interrupt. "I can't live without you. I don't want to. I don't understand what happened to me, and I don't know if it is permanent or temporary, but whatever control I have, I choose you."

The relief I felt was immense but not enough to completely overshadow my sadness at the loss of those I loved in my own time. I could survive that grief though. I didn't think I could survive leaving Gracen behind. And I knew that my family would understand. They would want me to be happy. And Gracen made me happy.

I apparently made him happy too because the moment the last word left my mouth, he picked me up, swinging me around. His lips were on mine almost instantly, hard and desperate, telling me without words just how badly the thought of losing me had scared him. I met his kiss with equal fervor, determined to make him understand that my need for him was as strong as his for me.

As he set me on my feet, his hands moved to the small of my back, pulling me closer, pressing our bodies together until I could feel him hard against my hip. His fingers moved up my back, over the outline of my tattoo under my shirt, reminding me that there were no more secrets between us. Whatever obstacles remained between now and our happy ending, we would face them together.

He pulled away, and although he was breathing heavily, he was clearly stopping us from going any further. My body was protesting, but my brain knew it was probably a good idea. Getting caught up in things might have felt really good, but we did have some other plans we needed to discuss before things got any more heated.

"What do we do now?" I asked as I clung to him, not trusting my legs to hold me.

"I have an idea."

"What's that?"

I frowned as he stepped away from me and then gasped when he went down to one knee.

He had to be joking...right?

He took my hand between his and squeezed. "Honor Daviot, would you do me the great honor of agreeing to become my wife?"

Shit. He wasn't kidding.

Chapter 28

This was what it was supposed to feel like. Palms sweating. Heart racing. Chest tightening until it was difficult to breathe. Complete adoration in the eyes staring at me. Electricity racing through my body from the point where our hands touched.

Not the casual, half-assed, "so I suppose we should get engaged for real this time" that I'd gotten from Bruce. Even his impulsive proposal after we'd slept together had been more romantic than the one that had actually gotten a ring on my finger.

Both times with him, I'd said yes, but I'd never felt the butterflies in my stomach, the tears welling up in my eyes. I'd said what was expected of me, what I thought I was supposed to say.

This time, I had no doubts, no questions about whether or not this was a good idea. I simply threw my arms around Gracen and squeezed a whisper past the lump in my throat.

"Yes! Of course, yes!"

His embrace was solid, comforting, making me wonder how I'd survived without it, how I'd survived without him. I didn't belong in this time, but I belonged with him. I had no doubt of that. I didn't care where or when I lived, as long as I was with him.

A gunshot in the distance snapped us both back to reality. It wasn't close enough for us to panic, but it was closer than I was comfortable with.

"We should go." Gracen sighed. "Better to keep moving."

"Moving where?" I asked.

"Away from Boston for now." He looked down at me and frowned. "Did you bring additional clothing?"

I raised an eyebrow and gave him a pointed look. "You do realize that your clothes look as bad as mine, right?"

He chuckled, an easier sound than I'd ever heard from him. He held out his hand to me and pulled me back to him again. "I would like to be able to walk with you and have people know that you are my fiancée, not my steward."

For another few seconds, I didn't realize what he meant...and then it hit me. I was trying to pass as a man. While not exactly commonplace in my time, any hint of impropriety between two men during this time period was a punishable offense. All it would take would be one wrong look or touch, and we'd be in serious trouble.

"I have a dress." I reluctantly stepped away from him and reached for the pillowcase I brought with me.

I reached for the hem of my shirt again and chuckled when he turned around. Such a gentleman. I swapped my uniform for the dress, frowning as I pulled it on. While I'd miss running water and some technology, the biggest thing from my time that I'd miss – aside from my family and friends – would be the clothes. Army uniforms weren't always the most comfortable things in the world, but they were a hell of a lot better than the shit women had to wear now.

When I turned back around and saw Gracen

watching me, however, I knew that being with him more than made up for the things I would no longer have.

I held out my hand to him, smiling at the look of warm surprise that crossed his face. He took my hand, and I threaded my fingers between his.

"Lead the way."

We walked for a few minutes before he spoke. "May I ask a question?"

"Of course." I had a feeling he'd want to know things about the future. I would have if I'd been in his place.

"That was your uniform?"

I nodded.

"Do all women in your time dress as men, or only ones in the military?"

I laughed and squeezed his hand as I tried to explain modern fashion, or at least my limited knowledge of it. I was always the kind of person who went by what I liked, both for comfort and style, rather than designer name or popular trends.

From there, we went around to other topics, prompted both by questions from me and ones from him. We spoke of our families and how we'd grown up. He told me more about Silva, and I told him about Bruce, though his answers were far more complimentary than mine. We talked about things to come, though my basic knowledge of history wasn't even close to enough to answer all of his questions.

We'd been walking for most of the afternoon when we found a small town. Well, in my time it would've been small. Here, it was a thriving community. Houses, a church, an inn, some small shops. I knew the city of Boston, as well as many others, would end the war with physical scars. This town appeared to be untouched, and I didn't know if it would stay that way.

A group of about half a dozen young children ran by, and I hoped that things here would stay as calm and innocent as they appeared right now.

"I want to marry you today."

The announcement, understandably, caught me by surprise. He turned toward me, his eyes blazing.

"Today?" I stared at him. I didn't know the usual procedure for wedding planning in the eighteenth century, but I assumed some things remained the same. Like who would normally be a part of such a day. "Don't you want your family there?"

My heart twisted at the question. No matter how long we waited, my family would never be there for my wedding.

"I only need you." He brushed the back of his hand across my cheek. "Why should we wait another minute? I want to make you my wife today, before anyone tries to stop us."

He was right, I realized. If we waited, things would come between us. His father. Clara. This war. Whatever it was that had brought me here. There were so many things that could stop us from being together. And no reason to put it off. Whether it be today or thirty years from now, I couldn't imagine loving anyone more, or having anyone love me more. I'd already decided to stay for him. This was only making it official.

"Okay, let's do it."

His entire face lit up at my words, and his eyes shone. I could get used to gazing into them. Losing myself in his eyes. He gave me a quick, breathless kiss.

"Wait here a moment," he instructed as he headed toward the building I'd already identified as the church, though what kind, I couldn't say. Considering when and where we were, I felt comfortable assuming it was some sort of Protestant denomination.

I'd seen similar things in Iraq. In the middle of a desert where houses were covered in dirt or sand, worn down, the places of worship were always gleaming, looking essentially brand new. The people cared for the temples with a respectful reverence I'd rarely seen in my own country. I pushed aside the thoughts before they could take hold. I didn't want to think about Iraq now, not on my wedding day.

My wedding. Even after years of being engaged to Bruce, it still sounded weird to think those words. I'd never been the kind of girl who spent hours daydreaming about her wedding, not even after Bruce and I had gotten engaged. My mom would occasionally ask me questions about if we'd set a date or thought about venues, and I'd seen her confusion every time I said we hadn't.

I pushed those thoughts aside too. If I thought about my mom, I would cry, and I didn't want to do that. Fortunately, Gracen was coming toward me, and that was enough to distract me. He wore a fierce, proud expression, and every step he took in my direction was a commanding one. Walking a few paces behind him was a man, and as they drew closer, I realized he was carrying a Bible. The minister. Who didn't look entirely too happy about being there.

As they got closer, Gracen started pulling at his clothes and hair, dusting off the dirt and trying to pull his hair back. It was such a stark difference from the coat and blue cravat he'd worn when his engagement with Clara had been announced.

I suddenly felt self-conscious as I realized that I was about to get married in a dusty, wrinkled blue dress. Without time to do something with my hair, it just hung down to my shoulders, as plain as always. I bent down and plucked a couple of flowers, as much to keep my hands busy as anything else.

Gracen smiled at me, an understanding look on his face. It occurred to me that while I'd never been married before, he had.

"I love you, Honor, and I wish to marry you today, but I understand if you don't want to. We can wait for something a little more...well, more." His tone was soft as he cupped my chin.

It took me a moment to realize that he thought I was regretting my decision because I wanted a big wedding. The truth was, I wasn't hesitant to marry him this way at all, just nervous. Marrying him just made everything more real. Made me acutely aware that I wasn't going back to my time. That I'd left it all so I could be with this man.

"I want to." I returned his smile. It didn't matter to me where we got married. Hell, I would've followed him to the ends of the earth if I had to.

He dropped his hand from my face to link my fingers with his, and we both turned to face the minister. The entire ceremony went by in a blur, and before I knew it, I had a beautiful silver ring on my ring finger and a new last name.

We'd gone straight to the inn to order some food and get a room for the night, and now we were sitting at a back table with two bowls of fairly suspicious-looking soup and some excellent bread. It was strangely awkward to be sitting at a table with my husband.

Hell, it was awkward to realize that I now had a husband.

Things were moving so fast that my head was spinning.

"Honor?" Gracen questioned, clearly concerned. "Are you well?"

"Yes, sorry, I was just thinking about things," I smiled at him, but I knew it didn't reach my eyes. I changed the subject before he could ask about it. "How did you get the minister to agree to marry us on such short notice? I don't know about now, but in my time, it usually takes some time to get a marriage license."

Except in Vegas, I thought. But I wasn't about to go there.

"Money can do wonders." He looked slightly embarrassed.

"You bribed a minister?" I put down my spoon.

I'd been taught from an early age the importance of fair play, of how people should be treated equally regardless of where they came from or who they were. I'd always despised stories of rich kids getting away with things when poor ones wouldn't have had the chance, and now I was married to someone who'd used his position and wealth to do exactly what I loathed.

"That's just the type of thing your father would do. Use money to get what he wanted." The words came out more harshly than I intended, and I regretted them as soon as he looked up at me, hurt in his eyes. I softened my tone. "I'm sorry. I just feel strongly about people not using their influence to get special treatment." I reached over and lightly touched his hand. "Even if it is done with the best of intentions."

"I only wanted to take care of you," he protested.

"I know." I tried to keep the frustration from my voice. "But I can take care of myself."

"I am aware of that." He lowered his voice, the admiration clear. "You've proven it a hundred times over." He paused for a moment, and then continued, "But you are my wife, and I want to take care of you, which is exactly what I will do. Because I can't lose you. I need you as much as you need me."

"Yes, *husband*," I said with a smile. It might've been old-fashioned, but I secretly loved the way "husband" sounded when I said it aloud. And I loved even more knowing that he thought of us as an equal partnership.

A comfortable silence fell as we finished our meal, but near the end, I found him watching me with a strange expression on his face. Like he had something he knew he had to say, but he knew that I wouldn't like it.

"Out with it," I said.

"What?"

"Whatever it is you don't want to say. Just say it."

He sighed as he took my hand. "We have to go back."

"Go back where?" I really hoped he wasn't suggesting what I thought.

"Back to my home to explain everything to my father." He gave me a partial smile. "And to introduce you as my wife."

Yeah, that was going to go over well.

And there was something else.

"You know at some point we'll have to take a side?" I said it as gently as I could. "And with what I know, there's only one side we can take."

He sighed. "I know." His smile widened. "But not tonight, because tonight is our wedding night. Any decisions we have to make can wait."

Chapter 29

The room he'd rented was large and simple with a small dresser, a few side tables and a jug of water. The bed was simple as well, but the sheets looked clean, and that was all I cared about at the moment.

Walking a few paces in front of Gracen, I stopped and looked over my shoulder. "Care to help me with this dress, Mr. Lightwood?"

"I would, Mrs. Lightwood."

I shivered, though I wasn't sure if it was from the name, or from the cool air as the dress slipped to the floor. I turned toward him, then chuckled at the look on his face. He clearly hadn't paid much attention to my undergarments before.

"It's called a bra," I said as I reached behind me to unhook it. "I'll explain later."

Gracen's eyes darkened as they slid down my body, and I let him look. There was no embarrassment, no hiding necessary. He knew all of my secrets.

"Your turn."

He shed his clothes quickly, never taking his eyes off of me. When he was naked, it was my turn to admire his lean muscles and tanned skin. I ran my gaze down his chest and stomach to the thick shaft curving up from dark curls. I licked my lips and heard

Gracen moan.

Then he was there, his hands sliding over me, cupping my breasts, teasing my nipples. He claimed my lips, his tongue exploring every inch of my mouth. I put my hands on his shoulders, feeling the strength there.

"Take me to bed," I whispered against his lips. "And don't be gentle."

He gave me a startled look that darkened the moment I caught his bottom lip between my teeth. His hands drew lines down my body, electrifying everywhere he touched and leaving every cell tingling. They finally came to rest on my hips, moving me backwards until I reached the bed. Without taking his gaze off of me, he pushed me back. I wrapped my arms around him, pulling him down on top of me.

A moan escaped me as our bodies pressed together, and my fingers dug into him. I wrapped my legs around his waist. The tip of his cock brushed against me, and I arched up against him. We had plenty of time later to explore, to learn all of the ways we could bring pleasure to each other. I just needed him inside me.

Now.

I ran my nails down his back until they reached his ass. I pulled him even as I lifted my hips, letting the first couple inches slide inside. He moaned my name, then cursed as he pushed the rest of the way into me. His muscles flexed under my hands as he began to thrust, starting with slow, deep strokes.

Time evaporated, and nothing else mattered as he moved against me, each time filling me more than the last. We'd had a connection before, but this was different. Some of it was because he was my husband because he'd made that forever commitment to be, even when he knew how many problems our marriage would cause. Most of it, however, I knew came from my confession. Now that he knew it all, that we'd shared our deepest secrets with each other, we could give ourselves freely, hold nothing back. As I begged him to drive himself into me harder, faster, I could see on his face that he understood it too. We didn't have to pretend, didn't have to worry about hurting each other. We were both strong, both fighters. We could protect each other, love each other. Equally.

My orgasm exploded through me, and I cried out his name, not caring if anyone else heard. I loved my husband, loved the pleasure that he was giving me, and I refused to be ashamed of it. He pressed his face against the crook of my neck, muffling his own groan as he reached his climax. My body tightened around him, muscles spasming as I came again.

One day, I realized with a start, this would give us a child. We didn't have access to birth control, no real way to keep me from getting pregnant. And the thought didn't concern me like it would have if it had been a different man spending himself inside me. The thought of a family with Gracen was a happy one.

He rolled off of me and pulled the sheets up over us. Neither of us spoke as we settled into the rapidly dimming light.

"I love you, Honor," he murmured as he kissed the top of my head.

"I love you too." I snuggled against him, letting myself relax in the safety and warmth of his arms.

I woke suddenly to a dark room, and was briefly disoriented, not recognizing my surroundings until the arm around me tightened, and I remembered where I was. And who I was with. I shifted, pulling Gracen's arm closer as I put my head back on his chest. I smiled at the sound of his steady heartbeat.

As I waited for sleep to come again, my mind turned to our imminent return to the Lightwood estate. I knew exactly how Roston would take the news of our marriage, and it wouldn't be pretty. I thought of Clara too and felt a pang of guilt. Then I remembered the selfish way she had tried to manipulate Gracen into joining the army because of how it would make her look. And the fact that the engagement wasn't one of love.

Not like this.

A bolt of fear went through me, and I pressed myself more closely to Gracen. I knew the dangers of what was coming, but it wasn't the war I was frightened of. Not really. I knew there'd be risks, but it was the true unknown that scared me. The unknown about what had brought me here...and what could send me home.

That wasn't home now though. My home was lying next to me, and I was suddenly terrified that I might lose him.

"Please," I whispered into the darkness. To what or who, I didn't know, but I didn't care. All I cared was that it didn't send me back. "Please, let me stay."

I listened intently until I felt sleep coming to claim me again, but no answer came.

The End

**The Lightwood Affair continues in Fear and Honor
(The Lightwood Affair Book 2)**

More from M.S. Parker

Fear and Honor
Make Me Yours
The Billionaire's Sub
The Billionaire's Mistress
Con Man
HERO
A Legal Affair
The Client
Indecent Encounter
Dom X
Unlawful Attraction
Chasing Perfection
Blindfold

Club Prive
The Pleasure Series
Exotic Desires
Pure Lust

Casual Encounter
Sinful Desires

Twisted Affair
Serving HIM

Acknowledgement

First, I would like to thank all my readers. Without you, my books would not exist. I truly appreciate each and every one of you.

A big "thanks" goes out to all the Facebook fans, street team, beta readers, and advanced reviewers. You are a HUGE part of the success of the series.

I must thank my PA, Shannon Hunt. Without you my life would be a complete and utter mess. Also, a big "THANK YOU" goes out to my editor Lynette and my wonderful cover designer, Sinisa. You make my ideas and writing look so good.

About the Author

M. S. Parker is a USA Today Bestselling author and the author of the Erotic Romance series, Club Privè and Chasing Perfection.

Living in Las Vegas, she enjoys sitting by the pool with her laptop writing on her next spicy romance.

Growing up all she wanted to be was a dancer, actor or author. So far only the latter has come true but M. S. Parker hasn't retired her dancing shoes just yet. She is still waiting for the call for her to appear on Dancing With The Stars.

When M. S. isn't writing, she can usually be found reading– oops, scratch that! She is always writing.

Made in United States
North Haven, CT
30 August 2023